Reviews for
Storied Moments - Book I Finders ... Keepers ...

"You think you will read just a few of these captivating short tales, but then you find yourself unable to put it down. Beautiful and intriguing writing about small moments and grand ideas, the great human experience accompanied by Joseph Cosby's marvelous images. Love the email exchanges which give another depth to the book and the moving relationship between these two friends... Has there ever been another book like this! Sit down and enjoy as you would a great meal."

– **Paul Elliott** Cinematographer, Director of Photography | Credits: Dark Winds, No Time for Old Men, The Sunset Limited, True Grit, Georgia O'Keeffe, House of Cards

"Masterful. Well Written. Great Read"

– **Tony Mark** Film Producer, Director, Screen Writer | Credits: The Hurt Locker, And Starring Pancho Villa Himself, Most Wanted, Vendetta

"Finders Keepers is a fascinating experience in the integration of words, pictures and memories. The pages compliment each other in a poetic thread that makes each one more vibrant than the last. But what makes this book stand out from all the rest is the unique relationship between the author and an old college friend that is portrayed in a series of letters between the two. What makes it even more fascinating is that they have not seen nor spoken to each other since they left college more than 60 years ago. The bound that still exists and the memories they share is both heartwarming and revealing. It also reminds us of the great lost art of letter writing. The book makes you feel, think and wish you had shared the journey that made it all possible."

Robert Martin Founding Executive Director of The Presidio Theatre, San Francisco | Former Executive Director & Artistic Director of The Lensic Theatre, Santa Fe

"Since Wednesday, I was supposed to mow the lawn, I was supposed to go to exercise, and my daughter has been hammering me for your book. Every time, when I read one of your stories - just when I think I know how it's going to end - it doesn't. I can't put the book down. The lawn and my daughter are going to have to wait. When do I get to buy Book II? I think I can afford it."

James Schreiner: Joseph's long-lost and recently found brother

Storied Moments is in many ways a unique work.

The reader will find stories of Geronimo, Anne Boleyn
Vladimir Putin, The Archangel Michael, Dante,
The Grail Knight, Mary, Rumi, Dostoyevsky,
and others of note.

The stories are
Historical, with more than a good dose of truth.
Spiritual, without being gnostic.
Absurd, while being totally believable.
Questioning the fabric of our lives,
While forcing no answers.

There are virtually hundreds of stories nestled within the
Vignettes, the e-mails between the authors, and the pictures.

Artfully woven in the stories and the
Correspondence between the authors are
Snippets of their lives as they each
Pulled from the other the gems now placed here-in..

The two authors first met and
Befriended each other during the two years
They were in college together. Many years would pass
Before they renewed and strengthened those bonds to produce

Storied Moments
Book I **Finders ...Keepers,** and
Book II **Losers ...Weepers**

As of this printing

They have neither seen

Nor spoken to one another

In more than 60 years..

No part of this book may be reproduced, or stored in a retrieval system,
or transmitted in any form or by any means, electronic, mechanical,
photocopying, recording, or otherwise,
without express written permission.

©Joseph Cosby

Santa Fe, NM

www.Storied-Moments.com
info@Storied-Moments.com
Joseph@storied-moments.com
Published by Storied-Moments
Narrated by Joseph Cosby

Cover design by Michael Campbell
Photography by Joseph Cosby (except where noted)

Print Hardback Version ISBN 979-8-9905997-0-3
Print Paperback Version ISBN 979-8-9905997-3-4
EPUB Version ISBN 979-8-9905997-2-7
Library Of Congress 2024917091

First Edition, November 2024
Printed in The United Sataes of America

Storied-Moments

Book I

Finders ...
Keepers ...

by
Joseph Cosby and
Dennis Thompson

Table of Contents

Forward
In the Beginning
Rhonda's House
Later

Chapter I

The Whippoorwill
Death Row Inmate
Visionaries
Ruminating
The Baby
The Duel
My Maiden Aunt
An Old Nazi Remembers

Chapter II

Anne Bolyen's Curse
The Queen's Consort
The Root Cellar
Haiku
Highballs at Sunset
Mississippi Chore Girl
The Instep
Cemetery Precautionary
Too Mean to Live

Chapter III

After the Ball
The Busker
Christmas Eve in Morocco
A Highlands Christmas
Granddaddy Death
Looks Twice
The Fairy Bride
Frankie
Seventeenth Summer
The Common Vernacular
Jeanine

Chapter IV
Her Longing
Three Pointless Pointillist Poems
The Transformation of Mary
In Need of a Wife
The Troubled Knight
Mary and Elizabeth
Suspicious Minds
Funny Girl
Time Traveller: India
Coroner

Chapter V
Appalachian Christmas Memory
The Dissimulator
The Settlement
Geronimo's Ghost
Housing Problem
Our Twins
Amanda
Brave New World
The Old Confederate
Dostoyevsky

Chapter VI
Rumi
Anne Boleyn's Falcon
Arkansas Traveller
Random Acts
The Vision
Queen of the Jukebox Rodeo
Her Letter
Broken Hearts
Summer's Colors
Step Mother
Soulmate
Haunted

The Authors
Introduction to Book II   Losers ... Weepers ...

Dedicated
to

Amanda and
Sheila

We heard
Your laughs,
Your Cries

As you
Read and
Listened to
our
Stories ...

the authors

Forward

If, perchance,
You might have wondered

What ever happened to
That friend of old,
That lost love,
That passer-by ...

You just might find them,
Or,
Someone like them,
In these pages

You will find the
Stories of Sinners and Saints;
Murderers and Thieves;
Cowboys and Indians; Gods and
Goddesses; Barmaids and Rascals;
Southern crackers and home-fried chicken;
Winds of Fire and Flooding Seas.

You will read of

People you know,
People you don't know,
People you don't want to know,

                        Ourselves …

all these stories are true
                        (well, most of them) …

****

It took Dennis and me
Most of our lives to write this book

Likewise, we hope that the
Reader pauses and
Ponders frequently,
As they explore these pages,
To wunder and wander.

Just as
Dennis and I have done
Before we finally put ink to paper

In The Beginning

These are the
Stories of and by
Two young men.

When they met,
One was in his third year of college
And the other was a freshman.

The older was a poet (and a scholar)
The younger was an artist and writer.
(And just a student).
Neither would know of
His or of the other's gifted talents
For more than half a century.

As loners, they had developed a bond.
But, when the older one finished his last year,
So too, ended their relationship.

Or did it?

The Diva

Prologue

Rhonda's House

Mondays are my workday off.
On Mondays, now and then,
I'll stop my car at Rhona's house.
Rhonda's house and Jim's.

Jim is at the mill today,
So, Rhonda says, *"Come in!"*
I find myself in Rhonda's house.
Rhonda's house...and Jim's.

I like the way that Rhonda says
"Sometimes...I need a friend."
That's why on Mondays, I stop by.
That's why she asks me in.

(An excerpt from the
complete poem,
contained herein)

Later .....

After Dennis graduated,
Each went their separate ways.

Dennis went to Arizona for a few years and then
Returned to his home town somewhere in the
Applachian mountains
To have a daughter and two grandsons
Where he remains to this day.

Eventually, Joseph wound up in
Santa Fe, New Mexico and continued life as an
Artist, author and professional photographer.

Dennis' wife of more than three decades
Had died of a massive stroke and
He chose to remove himself from the world by
Closing down communications with all but a
Limited few and even that
Only by mail or occasional e-mail.

For his social life,
He would sometimes have
Sunday dinner with his daughter and grandsons.

Then, entered the Muses.

It seems Dennis had been following
Joseph's photography career on his
Web site for several years,
Unbeknownst to him.

After more than 60 years of
Silence between them,
In late September of 2022
Dennis sent Joseph a
Short note to his web address indicating that
He *"might enjoy an occasional
Note from you."* (Joseph)
* * * * *

In an email a few months after
They started to work together,
Dennis wrote "*We had the threads of
friendship back then and
Over the years they became thin.
But never broken.*"

It seems that Joseph had long wished to use
His voice for something worthwhile and tho' he had done
Occasional commercials and voice-overs
He had given up hope of finding a "good script."

When Dennis sent him several of his "ditties" that
He wrote to amuse himself and his daughter,
Joseph saw something quite different than Dennis.

He wrote Dennis saying:

The soul of an artist is not
Something that is disciplined. It comes from a
Place within that compels the artist to use his craft to
Touch others and perhaps even the world in such a way that
Defies cognitive thinking and
Hones directly to their hopes and fears.

This is what your work does.
I now anoint you
Vignetteur-Extraordinaire. "

Would you listen to my
Reading of some of your work (begging apologies
For not having sought your permission) and
Let me know your thoughts?

Dennis wrote back *My work needed a voice.*
I accept your offer.

Such began their new relationship.

Still,
They have
Neither seen nor
Spoken to each other
In more than 60 years.

Chapter One

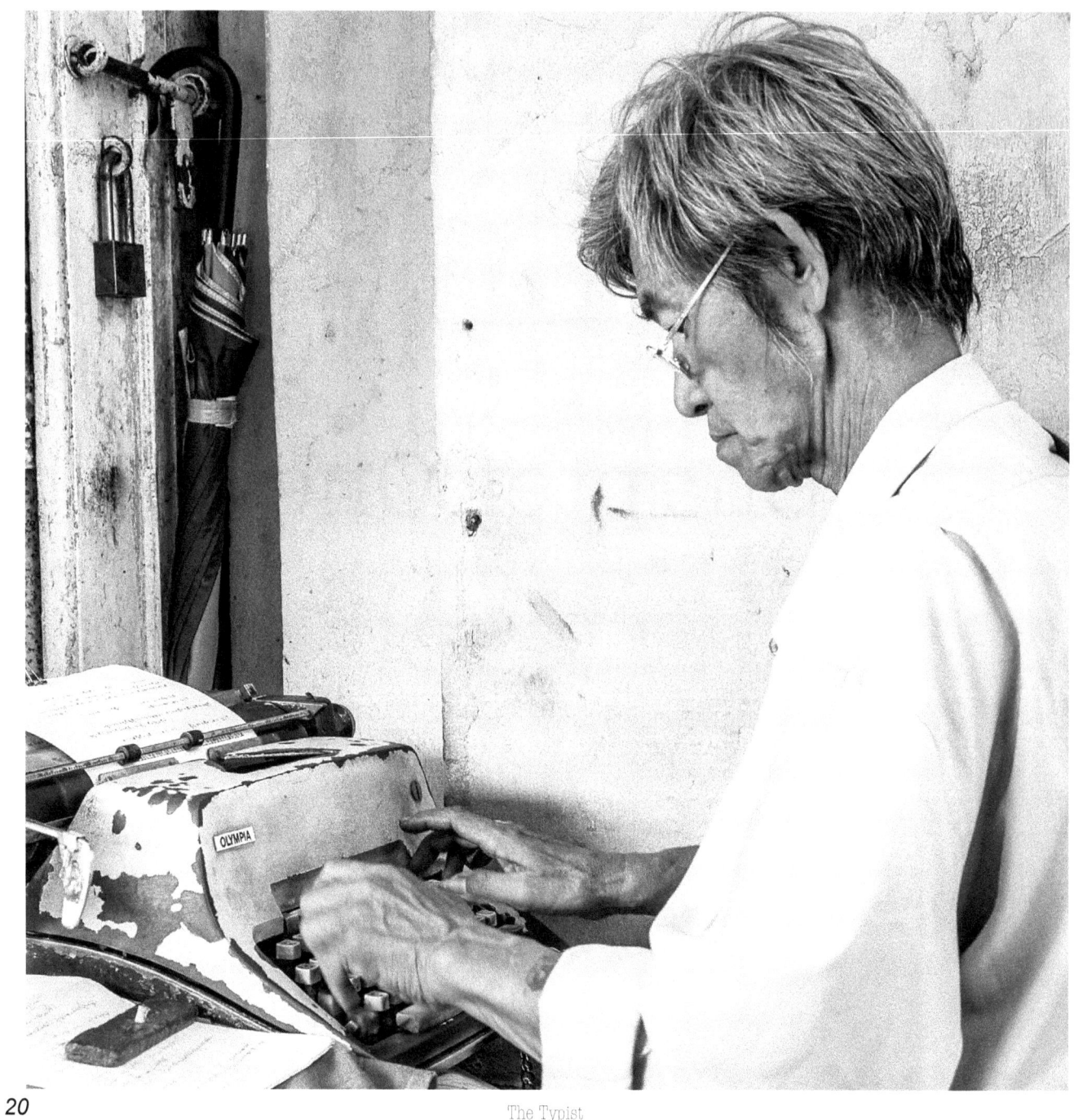

The Typist

From: Dennis
Subject: Touching base
Date: October 14, 2022 at 05:55 EST
To: Joseph

Joseph,
Thanks for replying. It is good to know that you are still out there, creating. From my limited research, it seems that you have developed an artistic genre pretty much your own. Perhaps a 21st century Ansel Adams?

The year 2022 is my 60th anniversary of graduating from Transylvania University (in Lexington, KY.) Recently, my thoughts have returned to those days. So many of our compadres have died, or otherwise become lost.

You are the only classmate that I keep up with. I traced down RH a few years ago, but when he replied to my email, he had me confused with someone from his seminary graduate school days.

When I turned eighty, I ended all telephone contact with the world, except for those business transactions that I can't handle over the Internet. I have also ended my in-person social life, except for an occasional dinner out with my daughter and two grandsons.

Essentially, I have become a monk, a recluse, a hermit —whatever term one might prefer. I made this life choice to preserve every possible minute for reading and writing and contemplation, given that my future years are in rapidly diminishing supply.

That said, if you drop me an email from time to time, catching me up on your life, I will enjoy it, and will answer — though it might take months.Since Evelyn died, (a final, massive stroke) I spend my time housekeeping, doing yard work, reading, and writing asymmetrical poetry — lots of ass and very little meter. Nothing that rises to the standard of modern poetry, therefore not publishable.

Thanks for being so creative and elevating the world profile of Transy graduates. We were fortunate to have experienced those years in that little University. Stay in touch, Dennis

The Whippoorwill

When I was five, and very small…
Just a lad, not yet grown tall…
Let's say some eighty years ago…
Let's call it 1944.

No air conditioned homes, back then.
You had to leave your hot bedroom
Those steaming Southern August nights,
And make your bed beneath the moon.

Those sticky Southern August nights!
Moon always full; air always still.
Fireflies, stars; sweet jasmine white.
(I'll frame my memories as I will.)

I would listen for a woodland sound,
From the hollow by the hill.
Three notes that were my lullaby;
The night call of the whippoorwill.

It called its own name: *whip-poor-will.*
From the hollow by the hill.
Those lonely, Southern August nights,
It called its own name: *whip-poor-will.*

Grown up, I left the sultry South.
Lived North and East and West as well,
But not once since those back yard nights
Have I heard a whippoorwill.

Some say that when we face our death,
Our lives will flash before our eyes
Like a fast-forward movie reel.
I'll ask for this scene; then... goodby:

The Hero: Small Southern boy...not more than five.
The Setting: A steaming August night.
The Mood: Full moon; sweet jasmine, white.
Soundtrack: By the Whippoorwill.

From its secret nesting place
In the hollow by the hill,
That lonely, long gone Southland bird;
Softly calling... *whip-poor-will.*

Maria Callas /Public Domaine

Death Row Inmate

In a way, he didn't mind dying,
But in a way he did.
He had killed the whole damned family
In a home invasion gone bad.

He had to give credit to his Warden,
Even if the Warden was a bleeding heart.
Well, I don't know. I just don't know.
His Warden's reply to his last request.

How about a t-bone steak supper?
Baked potato, shortcake and the works?
His good old Warden.
Just a conventional old-time Warden.

Dammit, Warden, you asked, and
I told you what I want.
I know we're expected to crave a steak,
But some men have other appetites.

No promises, his Warden had said.
I'll talk to the wife.
One of his favorite thoughts is of
The Warden's wife and her tight little britches.

But damned if they didn't pull it off,
The Warden and Mrs. Warden.
The needle was one of those
Damned square IV affairs.

The drugs were toxic, and
He could taste their metallic toxicity.
He settled his mind and stomach
As best he could.

And drifted on out to the sounds of
The Warner Classics recording of
Maria Callas singing Casta Diva, from
Bellini's Norma.

Act One.

From: Joseph
Subject: In response
Date: November 1, 2022 at 12:26 pm MT
To: Dennis

Dennis: I have read your note many times and have composed more that a few responses. So, I hope you are able to forgive my wanderings in this rejoinder.

Where to start? Over the decades, I kept only three names and numbers from our college crowd in my contacts.
1) Rick McCabe, we were roommates in freshman year and he left College at the end of his sophomore year (as I did) to join a Catholic religious order. That lasted for a day and he enrolled at Haverford to complete his undergrad. We hooked up in the early 80's and have witnessed the self-inflicted foibles and destructive paths our lives have journeyed, until there was finally the wheel of wisdom (or luck) that took control.
2) RH - I met him in Pueblo about 10 years ago and he had divorced from his college sweetheart and was winding up his ministry but still wearing the mantle. I found that tedious. We never spoke again.
3) Dennis Thompson -

I always wished that I had had more intelligence and self knowledge during that period we had together. I made up for that lack by being a bit of a smart-ass. But, you must have seen something deeper, which was not to appear for some time.

I, of course, respect your decisions about your hermitage, etc. But I would feel honored if I could send you my book. While you might have more than enough to read, Searching for My Lost Tribe - might be a journey few would want to take.

Without Sheila, my wife, I too, would be inward bound and the dogs would be my outlet. That I cannot imagine and I choose to spend little time contemplating that scenario, even though the odds are 50-50 it will come to pass.

Well, enough, so might you send me your address? I await your response.

Warmly, Joseph

A Hard Day's Work

Visionaries

Bust your asses! The Long Boss yells.
Trying to hurry up his work crew
So that they can knock off and
Get home for an early supper.

Dostoyevsky, either as an insult, or
Just because it needs doing,
Places his finger against his nose
And snorts out a stream of green snot.

The Long Boss takes it as an insult,
And cracks Dostoyevsky across the face
With his whip, causing Dostoyevsky's
Left eye to pop out onto his cheek.

Dostoyevsky finds that now he is able
To look at his own feet and at
The oncoming horizon at the same time.
Will this advantage him when he writes?
He thinks, probably so.

Blessed with his own unique attributes,
And living in London, Karl Marx
Witnesses this scene, and scribbles
Faster... before the vision fades.

At last, he can put down his pen.
Jenny! He calls. *Bring tea!*
I have written enough for today.
After, we will take a walk.

Epigram
Dostoyevsky is for dreaming, while Tolstoy rattles on.
Only Pushkin shoots the arrow straight.

Ruminating

While I await the Reaper, Lord,
My needs and wants are few.
To have good teeth and hot suppers,
And bowels that do what bowels should do.

To be awake at midnight
Beneath the full moon's glow;
To see the harmony of Natalie
Racing naked through the snow.

To have season's tickets, Lord;
Please see what You can do,
To guarantee my place in line
At Heaven's barbecue.

Well, that's quite the bucket list.
But, Lord, grant me one more thing:
To see violets in the meadows
Blooming random in the Spring.

A Sleep At Last

The Baby

It started life like any other baby.
Feeding at its mother's breast,
Its tiny hands, its trusting eyes,
Touching Mother's breast.

It was the year the crops failed.
What grain there was,
Was stolen by the ice pirates.
So there was no bread.

The grain gone, the bread gone.
The husband slain by the ice pirates,
The empty breast almost gone,
The mother did what mothers do.

She laid the infant on a pallet,
And stroked its parchment head,
Saying baby, baby, as she
Watched its soul retreat.

Yes, this is a sad little scene.
But remember, the soul is not dead.
It is simply in retreat.
Awaiting a more opportune time.

A year when the crops do not fail.
A country where there are no ice pirates.
Another mother, another breast.
Another quest for happiness.

From: Dennis
Subject: Visionaries (Take two)
Date: November 17, 2022 at 4:13 am EST
To: Joseph

As usual, your commentary inspired me to dig a little deeper…. Dostoyevsky and Marx were, in fact contemporaries, born within three years of each other, and dying within two years of each other. I had not known they were that close together until I started thinking about alternative names for my lead character.

Dostoyevsky works for me. If you do a narration of this one, feel free to change " Long Boss" to whatever works for you. I am happy with it, for now I am not sure about the phrase "oncoming horizon." Maybe needs to be a stronger term. I am trying to create an image of the future that is approaching us all, pretty much beyond our control.

Dostoyevsky's story is interesting. He was scheduled to be shot for his crimes, and just at the last minute, a reprieve from the Tsar arrived. Then he was sent to prison. Some theorists say that there never was an intent to shoot him, but the whole episode was to teach him a lesson.

I added the epigram just for a little spice. And because Pushkin, for me, is more fun to read.   Dennis

Two Old Geezers

The Duel

It's crazy to think that in the 21st century,
You could be forced into a duel.
But it happened to me.
Here's my story; every word is true.

My best friend, his woman, and I
Attended a Christmas dance.
I accidentally stepped on the hem
Of her trailing dress.

I held my foot there. Intentionally?
She walked on, and the dress ripped,
Exposing her e pluribus unum.
Obsequious apologies, but to no avail.

My friend would have satisfaction.
He challenged me to a duel. Me!
As the one challenged,
I had the choice of weapons.

Would I choose pistols? Epees?
For a moment I considered AR-15s.
But, in the end, I chose
Lily pads, at forty paces.

My friend...my ex-friend... was furious!
He remembered that I had been captain
Of the lily pad team at University.
But what could he do? Nothing.

We met on the green the next dawn.
We approached, sodden lily pads in hand.
For twenty minutes I slapped him silly.
Finally, he said, *Enough! I am satisfied*.

We fell into each other's arms and
Exchanged the kiss of friendship.
Then we repaired to a nearby bodega,
Where the friendly owner allowed us to:

Sit on a couple of inverted egg crates, while
We ate chips straight from the bags;
Dipped guacamole straight from the cartons;
And drank Tecate from quart cans.

The half naked woman, the cause of it all,
Long forgotten. The friendship restored.

Please remember this true tale —
This tale of Paradise lost and regained —

The next time you are challenged to a duel.

My Maiden Aunt

As a girl, she did her Mother's bidding.
She never served up hasty pudding.
Hands to yourself. Hands to yourself!
She kept her goods high on the shelf.

At eighteen, still a little green,
She let no man unzip her jeans.
Hands to yourself. Hands to yourself!
She kept her goods high on the shelf.

At thirty, *"Now it's time!"* she said.
She called up Ed and Ned and Fred.
But her goods remained upon the shelf,
For Ed and Ned and Fred were wed.

At fifty, she remembered Ted.
But Ted, she learned, was long since dead.
Hands to yourself. Hands to yourself!
Her goods, still waiting on the shelf.

At ninety, old Joe came around.
Said, *"Babe, let's put the hammer down!"*
Her answer was, "Oh, Joe, I'm tired."
My 'use-by' date has long expired."

An Old Nazi Remembers

Sausages

On that long-ago morning my frau and I craved sausages.
She wanted link sausages. I wanted patties.
So, we heated a 12-inch cast iron skillet
And filled it with sausages.

Linked, chewy, phallic sausages for her.
Round, comforting patties for me.
Hints of maple sugar; hints of sage.

We kept eye contact as we
Ate our… sausages.
Thinking, how happy we are!
As we ate our… sausages.

Not for one moment did we consider
The piglet, pulling on its Mother's teat,
Just an innocent little nuzzler.
It's destiny? To become sausages.

Not thinking of the porcine bonds
Being formed in rural
Schleswig-Holstein.
The look, the lust, the love.

Not for a moment, thinking of
The blind trip to the factory
Where sentient beings,
Having no say in the matter,

Would become … sausages.

February 13, 1945

We knew this night would come.
We did not know the precise date, but
Its coming was a certainty,
Because the war was lost.

And that is why we had kept her intact.
We secured her accommodations
In the finest suite in a guarded hotel.
Catered meals; anything she wanted.

We could not leave the City.
Dresden was ours to protect.
We would defend the City or die.
That we would die was a certainty.

How do you live when you know…
You know, without doubt, that
You will be dead within the month.
How do you carry on?

You will never see your wife again.
Your school sweetheart that you married.
The children that she gave you.
The children that you love.

We would dine with her, one by one.
Dressed in our finest uniforms.
Our medals polished.
Our Teutonic manners correct.

When I visited, we played
Her little gramophone,
Always Beethoven.
Often the Pastorale Symphony.

On another night, another Officer
Might ask her to amuse him with cards.
Or, one might request that she read poetry.
A few simply drank wine while admiring her beauty.

Men at war always capture women.
They make necessary use of these women.
The Japanese had their stables of
Chinese comfort women.

We had our women too.
Nubile, long-haired Jewish girls
Whose dark beauty far surpassed
That of our blond frauleins.

Our personal stable of mares,
To peruse, to use, to abuse, and
When we grew bored with them,
To be shipped to the camps.

They rode in cattle cars,
Those prim little Daughters of Abraham.
Once they were music students,
Readers and writers of poetry.

Now they were the cast aside whores of
The Master Race — the Third Reich.
No doubt most of them
Found their fates in the furnaces,
And welcomed the purifying fire.

But I was speaking of her.
The protected one.
The untouched, off-limits one.
The greatest beauty of them all.

Why can I make such a statement?
We had voted, you see.
When we sanitized the Dresden Ghetto,
We voted. She was unanimous.

I had assured her that when Dresden
Was safe for Jews to wander, she
Would be set free. We Officers had agreed
That he who molested her would die.

Then February 13, 1945, happened.
This was the night those who
Called themselves the Allies
Firebombed Dresden.

They turned our beautiful City,
The Florence on the Elbe,
Into a mass of molten steel
And ashes and bones and guts.

It was our night to die,
And we knew it.
The hundreds of air raid sirens
Ruptured our poor eardrums,

We, the Senior Officers,
Commanded the Junior Officers:
Hold your positions! Do your duty!
Defend our City! Save Dresden!

Then we repaired to her suite.
I myself was given the honor
Of gently rapping on her door.
And so I rapped, but gently.

When she opened the door,
Her countenance told me that
She was pleased to see me.
But then she saw the rest of us.

In an instant, she comprehended
Her final mission in this war;
For everyone in every war
Has a final mission.

And her mission in this war,
As even a fool could instantly grasp,
Was to distract us through the night,
While beyond these walls, our Dresden died.

Of all our little party, only I survive
To reminisce about that night.
When I think of her, I like to think that
She turned her mind to both the music

And the deafness of Beethoven.

The Beautiful Game

At Bergen-Belsen, 1943,
Our soldiers used the babies
For soccer balls. We cuffed the mothers
To posts and invited them to watch.

When a baby stopped screaming, a
Final kick to the head, and that was that.
Then a guard would toss in a fresh one.

Oh, I'm aware that the nickname
Came along after the Holocaust.
The Beautiful Game.
The Beautiful Game.
Having lived those days,
I could never call it that.

Footnote:

Bergen-Belsen was a Nazi Internment and Transfer Camp in Lower Saxony, Germany, active from 1941 -1945. The estimated death count at the Camp was 70,000 - 100,000. When the Camp was liberated by the British 11th Armoured Division, 60,000 half-starved prisoners were found inside. Some 13,000 unburied corpses were scattered on the grounds.
Source: Wikipedia.

The Beautiful Game is the poet's imagining. The footnote is reality.

CHAPTER TWO

Anne Boleyn's Dress

Anne Boleyn's Curse

I can no longer live my life
And not be cherished as your wife.
A wife to soothe your every care.
To twine her fingers in your hair.

A wife to feed your hawks and hounds.
A wife to lay her body down.
A wife whose body is weighed down
By your children, hale and sound.

To bear your children, fair and bright,
To hug and bless and kiss good night.
To keep the watch 'til morning's light
Is my Queenly duty and my right.

But since you've proven cold to me,
No babes of mine ne'er will you see.
At the ringing of the morning bell,
I'll be in Heaven or in Hell.

I yearn for Heaven or for Hell.
It matters not where I am bound.
And short lives for your future wives
And cruel deaths to your hawks and hounds.

Conquest of the Moors

The Realm Collection

The Queen's Consort

He whips out his penis as he approaches the Queen.
No Shakespearean trope can mellow this moment!
Head held high, swelling and swaggering.
His livery gleams golden in the honeyed light.

He, not afraid to shed blood to claim his birthright.
With a collective gasp, the attendants fall back.
Paralyzed by his daring, his lack of propriety.
Most of all, astonished at how small it is!

The Queen, glowing, preening, looks straight ahead.
Immobile, unblinking, quite unperturbed.
Hiding her pleasure, she was born for this moment.
Then, in the presence of the entire Court, it happens.

The assault: the penetration; the consummation;
The exhausted falling away.
In that instant, the trance is broken.
The Court surges forward, surrounding and buzzing.
From within the frenzied crush, the sounds of the slaying.
The limbs and head being ripped from the torso.

And who are the heroes and villains of our little melodrama?
Sir Walter Raleigh, four hundred years ago?
No! Just the honeybees down at the hive yesterday.
Doing what honeybees do.

History Footnote: Sir Walter's head was removed during the reign of James I, not Elizabeth I.

The Root Cellar

We kept him there
among the apples
In the root cellar
That winter
Because the root cellar
Was cold
But not freezing cold.

Kept him there
Among the apples
Until Spring
The winter soil
Too frozen
For a burial
Our Daddy.

Me and Little Sister
I'm Raymond
It was our job
To turn him
Once a day
Keep him fresh
Among the apples

Until the melting time
When he could
Be buried at the Church
The Words spoken
Daddy

Uncle Raymond came by
I was named for
Uncle Raymond
Daddy's younger brother

Tall, Black haired
Played the fiddle
Played the cards
Drank the liquor
Came by now
All the time for
Supper
Stayed late.

Came by now
To console Mother
Late into the night
Past our bedtime
Me and Little Sister
Cried

While Mama
Cried in a
Strange and savage
Way that was almost
Like a laugh.
Hands over
Little Sister's ears
When Mama's crylaugh
Got too loud
Four hands
God, I needed
Four hands.

That winter
That awful winter
The winter of
The frozen ground

Uncle Raymond
Dropping by
Bringing a chicken
Now and then
For Mama to cook

That freezing winter
The root cellar
Down the dark stairs
Me and Little Sister

Remembering now
The old times
Remembering
Uncle Raymond
Little Sister
Daddy
Mama
Mama.

Just me left
No wife
No kids
Just me
Remembering

The winter I stopped
Eating apples.

From: Dennis
Subject: Re: A Rose is a Rose, etc.
Date: December 1, at 3:25 am EST
To: Joseph

Joseph,
This is my morning for catching up on emails. Cathy's letter is compelling. Again, to your voice., if you ever want a second career as an Audiobook reader, go for it! Or another possible late-life profession — marriage counsellor — soothing the savage beasts that are in most of us.

Please share more of your readings, if the spirit moves you.

I can't get over the travel you have done, and the countries you have visited. Are you still traveling or are you stationed in Santa Fe for a while? When I lived in Phoenix, I knew a woman who worked in San Francisco, but who went home on weekends to Santa Fe.

I visited her there once. Her name was Charlotte Anderson. Possibly deceased by now (if not, in her 80's) or married and going by another name. Please check the Santa Fe phone book and let me know if there is a Charlotte Anderson listing (Old flames can't hold a candle to you....right?).

My days start at 1:30 am. I begin by working the crossword puzzle in the Washington Post. Then I work the Wordle and some other puzzles in the New York Times (All on-line). If I am successful, I assume that I have not suffered an overnight stroke, and then get on with my day.

All of my productive stuff has to be done by noon. My afternoons are devoted to reading and short naps. Not necessarily the schedule that I would choose, but the one that God has decreed that I must follow. And He knows best. All praise to Allah.   Dennis

Tatters

I
am here
for all to see

This is who
I am,
this is
me.

And yet -
a roll of
the dice,
a flip of
the coin

For, over there,
perhaps, in these pages,

could have been
my mother,
my father,
my brother,
my sister,
you,

me ...

from
Searching for My Lost Tribe
by Joseph Cosby

Tamales

Cathy's Letter

June 13, 2017

My Dearest Cathy:

I have written you many times-
but, I suspect you didn't get my letters.
You see, I am sure you forgot, but when you left,
you didn't leave a forwarding address or phone number.

How could you? You were only a few months old at the time and
I was only about two years old. .

We never met because I was already "placed"with
my adopted family and I didn't even know about you
until I was in the sixth grade.
Then, you would have been in the fourth grade, I guess.

Many years later my adopted mother told me that when
I was about two years old the Agency came by telling her that
my birth mother and father just had a baby girl
that was up for adoption and the Agency wanted to
keep siblings together, if possible.

It was the war years and my mother's husband was in Germany.
No one knew who would or wouldn't be returning home
when it was over.

It didn't happen.

I didn't even know your name until just a few weeks ago.
I am sure I saw you many times in those intervening years.

You changed a bit and you always seemed to age about the same as me.

You always had strawberry red hair (until more recently),
you were tall and had freckles. As you got older, you wore glasses and
your hair got a bit more blond.

It's funny how you always seemed to be there, wherever I was -
Washington, Paris, Kentucky, New York, Guatemala, Vietnam, Burma.

And, even though I would look at you across the street, in a park, at a
concert, on a train, you never seemed to want to talk with me.

So, I just kept on walking past. I guess it was just my imagination.

I digressed, sorry. Since I last wrote a lot has happened.

Just a few weeks ago, on my birthday, I met our oldest sister,
Janet, on the phone. She knew my given name - "Robert".
 She knew yours - "Cathy". She named her daughter after you.

She said she had been waiting for my call for the last 60 years.
I couldn't respond to that one.

After she did the DNA, we were certain that despite different fathers -
Ella Mabel (she preferred to call herself Mary) was our mother.

She knew all about me. For the first eight months of my life,
when she was six going on seven, she changed my diapers and
gave me formula - until they took me away.

Janet was already given away when you came along
but she did get to see you a few times before you were gone, too.

Back then, your mother, our mother, Ella Mabel, was
doing the best she could with six year old Janet,
three year old Jimmy and one year old Wayne -- when I was born.

All five of us, including you, were born in the same bed.

After I left home (I was eight months old then), our older siblings
would sometimes be at "home" and other times farmed out to relatives.

Their father was probably her husband, Glenn. By most accounts,
he was not a good man, not a good husband, not a good father.

I'll fill you in later on that. Forgive me Cathy, you want to
know about our mother, Ella Mabel.

Janet told me she died in the hospital in 1951 of cancer when
you were about seven and is buried in the family plot at the Pisgah
Cemetary in Nanjemoy, Md.

So, just as I am not sure who my father is, you are in the same boat as I.
It well could be the same. I am looking into that even as I write you.
I'll let you know when I find out.

But, if karma exists, and I think it does, you have had Janet and me
looking over your shoulder all your life.

We hope it made a difference.

Three Orphaned Siblings

Janet and I prefer to think that after all these years, we are brother and sister. The same for Jimmy. None of this "half" thing. Same for you. I am getting ahead of myself.

It seems that when Glenn, our mother's husband, came home from a year in the army hospital, he realized he could not have been the father of that two month-old child - me.

After I was taken away in late 1942 to be adopted, Glenn filed for divorce and Ella Mae moved to DC to look for work.

You were probably born in 1944 or 45 and there was another child just after you. We think she was put up for adoption, as well. And, there was rumored that yet another one followed her.

Back then, Wayne and Jimmy were passed around to different relatives, foster homes, institutions and then lived with Glenn for a while. That was not a good thing for either.

It seems Jimmy and Wayne had not spoken or seen each other since their early teens even though they lived only a few miles from each other. Wayne would have been 76 now, but I found out that he passed two years ago. Jimmy didn't know about that till I told him.

But, both married and had children and grandchildren.

Janet told Jimmy about me back in April when I called her. At first, he didn't want anything to do with me. Didn't want to talk with me and "just drag up nothing but bad memories", he said.

But, last week Jimmy told her that he is gathering pictures to
 send to me and said he will call me when he gets done
helping his daughter build a corral for her horses.

It's funny, every time the phone rings, I look at the
caller ID hoping it's Jimmy calling me from Pennsylvania.
Not yet.

The clock is ticking for all of us, so I hope he calls soon.

Janet told me that when she was little she always wanted a baby sister.
One afternoon when she came home from school in the early spring,
Rosie was there telling her that she now had a new baby brother.

Janet recalls she was angry and didn't want to go into the house,
And she told the doctor she wanted a baby girl. A sister. As all she had was
brothers. The doctor told her that all he had left in his bag was a baby boy.
Me.

That seemed to calm her down. She then went inside with Rosie
to see me and her mother.

When I spoke with Janet the other day, she hesitated at first and then,
 in a soft voice, asked
"do you think you can find Cathy?"

She didn't have to ask ...

Until then, your brother. Robert

© from
The Lost and Found Club
by Joseph Cosby

Highballs at Sunset

It was the fall of 1968.
Martin Luther King - killed in April.
Bobby Kennedy - killed in June.
We had the campus by the balls,
That semester of our rage.

Didn't we, Louie? Remember?
We were the Argyle Division.
Dressed head to toe in black.
Except for our argyle socks.

The night we put the bag of horse shit
On the Dean's front porch,
Doused it in kerosene and lit a fire?
Weren't we the rebels, Louie?

We didn't stay to watch him stomp it out.
It was on to the next aggression,
Where we threw half-full paint cans
At the Campus Chapel.

We had our demands, yes we did.
Didn't we, Louie?
Just like the first Martin Luther in 1517,
Nailing his ninety-five theses to the Chapel door.

Modern historians will disagree
Over Martin actually nailing his demands.
But the myth is alive.
The myth is all that matters now.

But we nailed ours. Our demands.
Nailed those suckers! Fifteen, as I recall.
What were they, Louie? Our demands?
Damned if I can remember a single one.

Mississippi Chore Girl

Janice was a big-boned, lank-haired
White-assed girl from Jackson.
And right out of high school, she got a job
As a Chore Girl with Angela's Angels.

She learned to do it all. Running
The grocery lists for the home bound.
Washing and turning Granny to
Keep the bed sores at bay.

Clipping the toe nails for
Four hundred pound bayou boys
Who haven't seen their feet in
Twenty years. Doing it all.

And then came the day that Angela
Called her in. *She's black. Old
Mrs. Forest is black. All the other
Girls have said no, Janice.*

Mother's Burden

*Everybody knows we don't take blacks.
But she called. Said she knows about
Our contract with the County. Says
We can't refuse her a once a week visit.*

*I'll take her on, Janice said.
Black, white, yellow, don't matter to me.
I'll give you a bonus, Angela promised.
A bonus will be fine, Janice answered.*

When she got there and rang the bell,
A washed and rouged black face in a
Starched white dress opened the door.
The house was spotless.

*I'm Janice, Janice said. I'm here
To do whatever. Right off, I don't
See much of a mess to contend with,
So where should I start?*

I want you to sit awhile with me,
Mrs. Forest said. *I live alone.*
So, let's just sit awhile and
Listen to the morning obituaries.

The next week, Mrs Forest
Started serving Janice with coffee and
Krispy Kreme Donuts. And they
Would sip and nibble and listen together.

Janice didn't tell Angela about
This piece of cake gig. Sitting and
Listening to the Friday morning obituaries.
Sipping coffee. Eating donuts. Nothing else.

The day came…don't these
Days always come? When another
Face opened the door. There was
No coffee. No donuts.

The obituary was lying in the front bedroom.
I'm Janice, Janice said to the daughter
Whom she had never met.
I'm the one who comes by.

*Well, thank you, Janice, but
As you see, you won't be needed any more.*

I've got a favor to ask, Janice said.
What is it, Janice? The daughter asked.

*I'd like to wash your Mama's feet.
And trim her nails if needed.
I offered to every week, but…
She never would let me touch her feet.*

Bare Feet

The Instep

If I were an artist, I would paint nothing but...
If I were a sculptor, I would sculpt nothing but...
Insteps.

That modest part of the human foot that
Attaches to the heel and gives the toes
Something to cling to.
The Instep.

A pleasant instep has a defined curvature.
A peasant instep is flat. And boring.
Women who endure the torture of high heels
Well understand the allure of arched insteps.

A fetish? I don't think so.
Toe sucking, now that's a fetish.
But insteps as fetish? My search of
The Internet has uncovered no evidence.

In fact, it's almost impossible to
Find attractive instep images.
Nothing to compare to yours, my dear.
You really could be a Vogue instep model.

Instep fixation (not fetishism)
Opens onto a field of possibilities.
I'll give you just one example...
Soundly based in history.

Instead of promoting worship of the Aten,
What if King Akhenaten had commanded
His subjects to worship Queen Nefertiti's instep?
Now, that they could have understood.

And Akhenaten would not have been
Erased from his rightful place in history,
And perhaps Nefertiti could have
Held on to the throne upon his death;

And her stepson, the Boy King,
Would have had to wait his turn.

With that Kardashian face, you just
Know that Nefertiti would have had
Insteps to die for. With arches
Like the domes of heaven. Yes! God!
Like the domes of heaven!

Cemetery Precautionary

Whenever you stroll through
Our little town's cemetery,
You had best watch where you step.
Some restless soul may have tunneled out
In the dark of night,
Leaving a six-foot deep hole.

Into which you, your head in the clouds, will fall
Face down into the empty coffin,
Which just happens to be a perfect fit,
Knocking yourself momentarily unconscious.
During which moment, two cemetery
Attendants will come by, and one will say:

Looky there, Billy Bob!
Some son of a bitch
Come by last night and
Uncovered old Mr. Johnson.
Probably to steal his Masonic ring.
Run over to the shed and get a shovel.

Billy Bob is small, but he is fast and efficient.
Back with a shovel in a flash,
Billy Bob will waste no time in covering you up.
Your family won't know where you went

Until you all meet in Heaven.

And what a tale you'll have to tell.

Luke 11:44. for ye are as graves which appear not, and the men that walk over them are not aware of them.

Two Angry Berbers

Too Mean to Live

That was me, age ten.
A kid too mean to live.
They should have made me
Wear a sign:
This kid is too mean to live.

That was the year that I told
Annie May Dalton that I
Was going to throw her
Down the outhouse.

And I might have done it
If she hadn't run home.
Annie lived next door in
A little rental shack.

Annie and her father, Raymond,
And a mother who I never met,
And a few extra kids who I
Never met. Just Annie May.

She was either a year older than me,
Or a year younger, or the same age.
And as blonde as a button.
Not albino blonde, but
Snow princess blonde.
That whiter shade of pale.

Annie May and I went on a date.
My dad took us to the picture show
To see Song of the South.

During the movie, he had to take
Annie May home because she
Was crying. When my dad came back,
He said, *She had to go to the bathroom.*
And she refused to come back to the movie.

My memory of Raymond is the time
That he did some work for someone
And they paid him off in watermelons.

When he came home the entire
Back seat of his old car was
Loaded with watermelons. And he
Didn't offer me one. Not one.

And after me taking Annie May
With her undersized bladder
On a date to see Song of the South.
And after me
Not throwing her down the outhouse
Like I should have.

I don't know why I was so mean
To Annie May, but that's the way
It is with serial killers, too. They don't
Know why, either. There's really
No point in putting them in analysis.
Just make 'em wear a sign that says
Too Mean to Live.

Chapter Three

After the Ball

The Senior Prom is over
And my baby doll is sitting
Across the kitchen table from me
Crying her eyes out.
(No, I don't care if you listen in.
Help yourself.)

He says he loves me, Mama.
But he danced six dances with
Mary Belle and he danced five with me.
I counted, Mama. I counted.

My baby doll is reduced to
Counting dances to see if she is loved.
But I can see why, Mary Belle being
His ex-girl friend, and all.

I confronted him, Mama.
You heard us on the porch.

Oh yes. I heard them.
Heard him saying, *But Jenny.*
But Jenny. Over and over.

He said Mary Belle asked him, Mama.
Does that make it different, Mama?
He could have said "no".
But he said "yes", Mama.

I put my left elbow on the table,
Then put my chin in my hand
Like my mama used to do,
To see if it would help me think.

How do you give advice in a
Lover's quarrel without making
Matters worse?   Maybe my listening
Is all she really needs.

And she's got that pretty name, Mama.
Mary Belle. And I'm just Jenny.
That's what you call a mule, Mama.
And you and Papa named me Jenny.

And, of course, that's when I had to
Speak up. Your name's Jennifer, honey.
Jenny is just a nickname. Now,
You know that. Would it help if
We started calling you Jennifer?

It might, Mama. It just might help.
There's lots of movie stars named
Jennifer, and they are all pretty,
And they don't go by Jenny.

Then that's what it will be, Jennifer.
I'll get the word to the family.
And I'll tell your teachers.
You'll have to tell your friends.
And start with telling your boyfriend.
Jennifer it is.

At last, a smile. Now she has a
Plan. Something to go forward with.
Something to help her deal with
This frustrating man. And aren't
They all frustrating?

What I would like to do is go
Over to his house, call him out
In his front yard, and give him
 A royal ass whipping.

That's what my mama would have done.
Did, in fact, do a few times.
But you don't do things like that
 In these modern days.

I tell her to blow her snotty nose
And dry her eyes, while I pour
Both of us another cup of coffee.
I find that coffee cures most things.

The Busker

She opened her battered guitar case
And set it on the sidewalk.
Unfolded her battered camp stool and sat.
Cradled and tuned her battered guitar;
Wearing her battered cap, coat and jeans.

Her guitar was missing a string,
Causing her to skip a few notes,
Which went unnoticed by those few
Who stopped to listen.

A small audience, but, no matter.
A few of the few
Dropped dollar bills into her case.
One guy dropped a Hamilton.

Which meant that Carol,
For such was her name, ate supper
And had a room and a hot bath
At the local Motel 6.

Which meant that those few,
Those happy few,
Their consciences freshly burnished,
Felt a warm glow that Christmas Eve.

From: Joseph
Subject: Good Tidings, etc
Date: December 22, 2022 at 2:25 pm MT
To: Dennis

Dennis: I think I will be "slaving" this Xmas. Working on your masterpieces. Well, at least it keeps me out of the bars and chasing "doves" in the back forty.

I was thinking of those decades ago (when I got thrown out of the history department in my senior year) of changing my major to a language major. BUT, that would have required two math courses. I had everything else needed. But, math was definitely NOT my forte.

Even so, I can still do some simple stuff, such as add and subtract. So, I am wondering HOW, you have a grandson of such a young age? And it appears you haven't gained a pound in all those decades. You might have called that last ditty - "The Last of the Mohicans".
Stay warm, Joseph

****

From: Dennis
Subject: Re: back then
Date: December 23, 2022 at 3:25 am EST
To: Joseph

Now, this is interesting. One of the reasons that I chose Transy is that I could scoot through without a mathematics requirement. You and I were alike in our resistance to the numbers.

Glad you are enjoying the poems. It is nice to send them to someone who catches the humor and other nuances. I have a daughter-in-law who becomes alarmed at some of my poems, and she calls me to see if I am depressed. I assure her that I am not.
Dennis

From: Joseph
Subject: Troubled Knight
Date: December 24, 2022 at 10:02 am MT
To: Dennis

You know that when I arrived at the doorstep of Transylvania, I realized that I was an outsider, surrounded by Southerners beholden to Robert E Lee and Christians. Is there a difference? BUT, in an unusual state of forbearance, I knew never to let on to anyone. my true feelings.

 I am thinking about the accent that would work best for Redneck. In the old days, I could do a good southern accident (whoops, that was accent) , but only after a shot of Kentucky's finest. I ain't got none of that stuff but I'm more than willin' to give it a shot.

Wadda' ya think about the Troubled Knight?

* * * * * * * *

From: Dennis
Subject: Re: Troubled Knight, etc.
Date: December 24, 2022 at 1.06 pm EST
To: Joseph

There, my friend, you have a challenge. There are so many variations in Southern and Appalachian and straight-up Redneck dialects. I will try to find a few poems that lend themselves to the variations.

I will send you another Grail Knight poem — the Berry Maid — which I tailored a little today. I enjoy writing the rhythms that the Grail Knight demands of me.

Berber Nomad

Christmas Eve in Morocco

It was not her holiday, my Moroccan beauty.
What did she know of manger scenes?
Of holy babes? Of wise men?
Shepherds in the fields? Now, these she knew.

On that Christmas Eve of starlit skies,
Our tent was buffeted throughout the night
By the sound waves caused by the
Berbers screaming from the dunes.

Enjoy your night of lust, young Englishman!
Revel in your carnal transgressions.
In the morning you will die
The death of a thousand dogs!

The death of a thousand dogs?
That old chestnut?
Is that the best they've got?

And yet… it caused me pause.
Sent a shiver through my liver.
Drained the swagger from my dagger.

This will not end well.

My personal lamp genie had warned.

There will come a time of deep regret…
There are lines that must not be crossed…

Even by bold young Englishmen.

A Highlands Christmas

She's been at cookin' all day long.
The mutton roast, the Christmas scones.
The supper eaten, her husband stands,
And sets to leave her all alone.

Good, my Love! Where gang ye now?
Where gang ye on this Christmas night?
I'm off to hunt the forest stag.
I shall be home about daylight.

Her Love has gone to hunt the deer.
But, ah, she takes a look around.
There in the corner stands his gun.
There by the fireside sleeps his hound!

Without his gun? Without his hound?
She tries her best to understand.
How will he slay the forest stag?
Will he choke it with his hand?

She follows him through dripping woods.
She follows him down paths so drear.
He enters a small cottage, drab.
No doubt a doe is dwelling here.

At the window, she peeks in.
And there! The scene she did most fear.
A pretty maid, a youthful maid…
Entwining with her husband, dear.

She must decide, now, what to do.
This man, to her, is bread and life.
She's gutted many a deer before.
She's brought along her gutting knife.

f

Granddaddy Death

Granddaddy Death went galloping, galloping,
On his inky black charger.
His faithful Midnight is forty hands high.
There is nowhere a horse that is larger.

Granddaddy Death wears a long black cape,
And he'll fold up your babies within it.
He'll say to the Missus, Here's veal for the stew.
Be sure to put plenty within it.

Granddaddy Death's on a mission tonight.
He's heard there's a bullfight in Spain.
This time, he is going to take the bull's part;
Ah, the tears that will fall like the rain.

He thinks he might stop in Paris, as well;
And gather a dozen young lasses.
And he might even snatch up a stray priest or two,
Just in case the young lasses need Masses.

And then it's to Belgium for dark chocolates;
The kind that the Missus is craving.
At last, at his fireside, his evening's work done,
For a nightcap with Poe and his raven.

Apache Spirit Dancer

Looks Twice

If you would optimize your time on Earth,
You must become acquainted
With your mythic self.
My mythic self is named Looks Twice.

Tonight I am taking supper with
Old Bear Claw, my grandfather.
We are dining on parched corn
And strips of dried buffalo.

Powder Woman, my grandmother,
Comes in, refills our plates,
And wrinkles her nose, before
Drifting out again.

Grandfather is telling me of the time
Of broken Earth, when our people
Climbed to the surface from
The boiling world below.

After supper, we will wander
Through the camp, and will
Speak briefly to Little Tumbleweed,
Who is crouching in the dust.

If you come too near, he will
Throw dust on you. Dust is
Easily brushed away. He
Belongs to the tribe.

Old Bear Claw tells again
The story of my father, who
Fell in battle before my feet
Even touched the Earth.

On our walk, we quickly
Skirt by my Mother's tent,
Where I am not welcome tonight,
Because Mother has a suitor.

I am tempted to spy on them,
To study his intentions, but
As soon as we finish our walk,
And smoke the pipe,

It will be time for me
To return to the world
Where I am no longer
Looks Twice.

The Fairy Bride

The Morning

She is back home from the wilderness.
The forest gloom; the bower room;
This elfin maiden fair.

Last night she danced naked in the glen.
The moon grown old; her skin so cold.
Her frosted raven hair.

This morning finds her dressed in fresh attire.
The gingham shirt; the modest skirt.
Her favorite opal ring.

Her husband finds her busy at her loom.
Her human life? This good man's wife.
He does not suspect a thing.

The Night

Last night she brewed his evening tea
With chamomile and something more;
He had no need to know what for.

He did not need to know his bride
Would leave his side at eventide
To roam the woodlands far and wide.

No need to know she sheds her clothes
For ivy vines and cedar boughs.

No need to know with cheeks aglow,
She sprigs her hair with mistletoe.

No need to know the Goat-God Pan
Will visit her time and again.

The price she pays (it does no harm)
To spend her days in human form.

His fairy bride.

Tangueros

Frankie

As soon as her shift ends at three on Friday afternoon,
Frankie is outta here. Says a *have a good weekend*
To the older women, and a *see ya later*
To the girls her age. Friends from high school.

She goes home to Mama's and says *hey* to Mama.
Then she goes into the bathroom and sponge bathes
The smelly parts and puts on fresh roll-on and scent.
She'll take an all-over bath, maybe, on Sunday.

By four she's at the Dew Drop Inn.
A bar with a little stage and a dance floor.
And enough tables to make it a restaurant, too.
Friday and Saturday nights, it's mostly a bar.

She likes to get there early, before the action starts.
She takes ownership of the place by roaming from
Barstool to table, and then back again.
Frankie is a regular and at home at the Dew Drop Inn.

Her tight little body is packed into her jeans
Like summer sausages. Her skinny arms pop
Some pretty good biceps, from all that lifting
And tugging at the mill. She wears penny loafers.

When the Sun goes down, the dancing starts.
Frankie will be dancing with a man she likes.
It doesn't matter if he is wearing a baseball cap
And a white t-shirt that almost hides his hairy armpits.

To bring their torsos into alignment, he will hunch over,
And Frankie will reach up and place her right arm tight
Around his neck. You would find it hard to
Slip a chewing gum wrapper between their bodies.

In an hour or so, you might see Frankie dancing
The same way with another good old boy.
Frankie is playing the field on this Friday night,
Because her heart is broken, since just last weekend.

The good old boys know that Frankie is in recovery.
So none of them push her too hard, knowing that when
She is ready for some good man's loving, she will give
The signal. Tonight, they are content — well, not content —

But reconciled that all they are going to get from Frankie
Is some slow dancing, and some feeling of her body, which
She does not resist. A chance to spend some money
Buying her drinks, while showing sympathy for her break-up.

There will be another weekend — perhaps next weekend —
When Frankie's heart will have mended enough to make a
Selection from the available good old boys, and
Take an extra one home for Mama.

Seventeenth Summer

When she grew old enough
To form opinions of her own,
She began thinking that farm life was not for her.
By age seventeen, she had no doubts.

She planned for this to be her last summer at home.
In the fall, she would start her senior year.
Next May, she would graduate,
And then she would be gone.

English, bookkeeping, typing, shorthand, French.
High School had prepared her well.
She could get a secretary's job in any city.
The resume entry, "French," might offset her Southern drawl.

So, this would be it — her last summer working on the farm.
Helping the family raise the tobacco crop.
Setting the plants, hoeing the rows, sweating, thirsty, sunburned.
Squashing the tobacco worms under her tough bare feet.

Riding the "slide" pulled by their antique mule, Ben.
Picking the gummy leaves, itching, poisoned by the nicotine.
Then under the shed stringing the leaves onto sticks.
And placing the heavy bundles into the curing barn.

And her constant struggle to avoid Jim's hands.
The hired man, whose help they really needed,
But who couldn't keep his hired hands off
Her seventeen year old sweetness.

Since they needed Jim's labor, she bided her time.
The last day of the season, she let him corner her, alone.
She pushed against him and put her hand over his mouth.
Then stuck an ice pick in his ass.

If you say one word, she said,
I'll tell Daddy what you've been trying to do.
No, Rhonda had no fears of life in the city.
Ice picks could be bought in any kitchen store.

Willie Nelson's Post Office/Store

The Common Vernacular

I'm gonna whup yo' ass!
There was a time, not that
Many years ago, that you
Would hear this statement
At least once a day as you
Moved through polite society
In the rural upper South.

Yes, I actually typed the
Above sentence without
Triggering the alarm bell
On my spell check, thereby
Proving my point.

But not so much anymore.

Times are changing.
Oh, you will still hear
Folks say *you'uns* now and then.
But you almost never hear
Us'uns. That's progress
Of a sort, isn't it?

But I miss hearing
I'm gonna whup yo' ass.
It reminds me of my friend Bobby Sam,
Who, believe it or not, served as
County Commissioner in
Jomeokee County for
Some twenty years.

Enough years, I suppose, to
Say *I'm gonna whup yo' ass*
To a majority of the voting citizens,
Because in the twenty-first year,
Bobby Sam lost his bid for re-election.

It broke him, losing the title of
County Commissioner.
I would visit him, try to tell him
Jokes, but he wouldn't laugh.
Finally I stopped going around.

Bobby Sam took to drinking moonshine,
And his run of luck continued, and
He got into a bad batch, and died.
The good old boy he bought from
Had run low on his hundred proof,
So, not wanting to miss a sale,

He had cut his supply with some
Radiator fluid, which was readily
At hand. This is a common
Practice, but he got his
Proportions wrong, and killed
Old Bobby Sam.

I miss Bobby Sam...
Just one of the old timers
Who helped keep the local
Vernacular alive and in circulation
With his *I'm gonna whup yo' ass*.

But good old Bobby Sam
Served his constituency until the end.
Leaving this world as a warning
To all the County's young bucks.
Don't drink radiator fluid.
City folks call it antifreeze.

Loaded

Jeanine

Today I visited a roadside convenience store
To pick up some chocolate milk; I'm into
Midnight milkshakes these days.

Jeanine was the clerk. She did not wear a name tag.
She did not say her name. I did not ask.
But when I left, I knew that I was leaving Jeanine.

If you have ever lived in the South;
If you have ever been a tourist in the South,
You may have encountered my Jeanine.

Jeanine is a subset of Southern womanhood
Who does not say, *Well hey, Sugah* ! when you
Enter her store.
You will often hear that said in the deep South.

When you have selected your purchases,
And paid your bill, my Jeanine does not say,
Thank ya, Darlin'. Ya'll come back, now.
That's how it's said in the Appalachian South.

When I entered the convenience store,
I said a pleasant *Good morning.*
The clerk did not respond.

I had to walk every aisle of the little store
Looking for the milk; past the snacks,
Past every flavor of soda pop and
Every brand of beer that God has created.

Finally, in a dark little corner of the store,
There was the milk. I grabbed a
Couple of bottles, and went to check out.

Please notice that while I was roaming
The aisles, a little lost puppy, the clerk
Did not come from behind her counter
And say, *May I help you, Suh?*

So, I placed my bottles on the counter,
And I said, I found what I needed.
No response from Jeanine.

Paying by credit card, I asked,
Is this machine a swiper or a tapper?
Nothing from Jeanine.

Oh, by the way. Jeanines have a
Body feature that is a dead giveaway.
Jeanine may be slim or curvaceous.
Jeanine may be blond or brunette.
I have never encountered a red head.

But every Jeanine that I have met
Has jowls. Not caused by baby fat,
But by that pursed little mouth
That has never cracked a smile.

Oh, and she will have eyes, often blue,
That constantly are peering into
Some far or middle distance.

Do you want your receipt? Jeanine asked.
Well, yeah; what are you going to do with it?
Wipe your ass? No, I did not say that.

Jeanine made no move to bag my purchase.
I was supposed to walk out with a
Cold bottle of milk in each hand.

Leaving the store with my milk,
Bagged at my request,
I thought, I'm in love with Jeanine.

I want to have a first date with Jeanine.
I want see where our conversation goes.
I want to try for a good night kiss.

A final word: If your name is Jeanine,
Please know that I have not described you.
I'm talking about the other Jeanine.

The one who waits for me,
And can't wait to wait on me,
At a little roadside market in the South.

From: Joseph
Subject: Wanderings. Good, Bad and the Other
Date: December 29, 2022 at 10:40 pm MT
To: Dennis

I would like to think that I am not judgmental. This project we are doing, whatever we might call it, brings out "stuff".

So, last evening, I trotted out "Christmas Eve in Morocco" to a couple who came over for wine and such. These are folks whom we have known for years.

Over the last years, I have been steadily examining my willingness to have relationships (at almost any level) with those in whom I find lacking that "Something" that I have not been able to label.

So, I did the reading. I did quite fine, if I must say so myself. The response was (from both) an almost blank stare.

"So", I said. "What do you think?" "*I don't get it.*"" they said.

So I let the husband read it, thinking my accent threw them off..
He said, "*Oh, I get it , it's about terrorists?*"

He wasn't kidding.

For a moment, I was stunned. I doubt they picked up on that.
I still don't have the name for that "something", but I know it when I see it and my "something detector " nails it.

So, in the time left to me, souls such as yours are precious gems.
Such is me thought for the day.

Joseph

Rhonda's House

Mondays are my workday off.
On Mondays, now and then,
I'll stop my car at Rhonda's house.
Rhonda's house, and Jim's.

Jim's my fishing buddy,
My Saturday best friend.
We plan our day while Rhonda
Scoops our coffee from the tin.

Jim is at the mill today,
So, Rhonda says, *Come in!*
I find myself in Rhonda's house.
Rhonda's house and Jim's.

She smiles and says, *Sit down.*
I'll scoop some coffee from the tin.
I'm sitting at the kitchen table
In Rhonda's house again.

I like the way that Rhonda says:
Sometimes… I need a friend.
That's why on Mondays, I stop by.
That's why she asks me in.

Chapter Four

Worries

Her Longing

More times than she can remember,
She has asked herself, *why do I love*
Such a thoughtless person?
Does he love me at all?

Their relationship was the result of
One wild night of passion.
A night she will never forget.
Yes, that night was the beginning.

Their early months were difficult.
His impulses were brutish.
The slaps, the occasional bite.
His fixation on and violence to
Her breasts.

Tiring of both the slaps and the breasts,
He moved on to other torments.
And yet, she stayed the course,
Freely giving her love.

They entered their happy years.
The years of him and her.
To hell with the rest of the world.
Fond memories of those years.

And then the arc of their happiness
Took a turn. No longer interested
In violence, and finding her company
To be a bore, he became neglectful.
These days she longs for his attention.

And now, we come to today.
Their years together have not ended;
Although in so many ways they have.
Today, maybe today, she thinks,
The Mother's Day card will come.

Three Pointless Pointillist Poems

The Considerate Poet

Some readers relish a risqué poem,
So, now and then, friend, you risk such a poem.
If the church ladies say, *Let's pray for this sinner.*
Then, two to one odds, you've written a winner.

Still, I always keep their sweet natures in mind.
And never write 'ass' if I can rhyme with 'behind.'
I never use x-rated 'shit' 'damn' and 'hell'
If 'doo-doo' or 'ca-ca' will work just as well.

Yes, I always keep the church ladies in mind;
I'll tiptoe up to it, but not cross the line.
I often write 'but' but I never write 'butt.'
You'd best use discretion when dealing out smut.

Too Much

In their eighties, they moved in together.
And why not?
An honest to gosh widower.
A chirpy widow.

The whole church noticed,
But no one said anything,
The kids — one his, one hers —
Were a different story.

They had them over for dinner.
They confessed, *We're doing it.*
Biff, who had gone to State,
Went outside and threw up.

Carol, the Vassar graduate,
Handled it better, as you
Would expect, since she
Had majored in poise.

Carol simply said, *Ewww.*
And, of course, they weren't
Doing it at all. They simply
Wanted to shock the kids.

An American at the Ball

I attended the Vienna Opera Ball of 2023.
And understood not a word anyone said.
How do they do it, those Viennese?
Speaking their perfect German?

Oh, someone said, '*aber*,' and
I knew the conversation was about to shift.
And someone uttered the all-inclusive '*und*.'
But beyond that… pretty much lost.

The Viennese waltz?
Now the waltz, I understood.
The dance needs no translation.
We share the language of the dance.

No one gets left behind.
Not even the gauche American
Whose ears stuck out much too far
That night at the ball in Vienna.

From Joseph
Subject: Death Row
Date: January 08 , 2023 at 12:39 pn MT
To: Dennis

I just whipped this off. I should do it a bit slower. BUT, do you want more drama in the voices? I thought keeping it on the lighter side was a nice juxtaposition to the gravity of it all, and then there was the ending. JC

****

From : Dennis
Subject: Casta Diva
Date: January 08, 2023 at 11.01 pm EST
To: Joseph

Casta Diva is Italian for Chaste Goddess, or Virtuous Goddess. Norma was a Druidic Priestess, and she is singing to the Moon Goddess, asking for many things.
If I were a dying convict, it is exactly the song to die to. I'm going to request it, even if I'm not a convict.
Safe Journey.
DT

* * * * * * * * * *

From Joseph
Subject: Death Row
Date: January 9, 2023 at 9:39 am MT
To: Dennis

So , when I say Act 1, there should follow about 15-20 seconds of Maria singing that piece and slowly fading out. (Just like we all will) n'est pas? Porque no?
JC

* * * * * * * * * * * * * *

From: Dennis
Subject: Re: Death Row
Date: January 9, 2023 at 7:45 am EST
To: Joseph

Go for it. She really is to die for.

From: Dennis
Subject: Re: Rumi 2
Date: January 11, 2023 at 4:19 pm EST
To: Joseph

Excellent! The cadence is just right. Our little corrections have improved it. I have no additional recommendations for improvement.

Amanda listened, and said the reading is exceptional. It is an old poem of mine, so she is pretty familiar with it.
When I suggested the concept of a book of poems, pictures, and a cd slipped into the back cover, she said to put her down for a copy.
Are any of your international acquaintances amateur poets? Would be fun them on board. Might even open an international sales market.
DT

* * * * * * * * * * * * * * * * * * *

From: Dennis
Subject: Rumi
Date: January 11, 2023 at 7:09 pm EST
To: Joseph

That one gives me shivers. Especially the final stanza. Thanks for the change. Very unpoetic of me to miss that. I have just changed the master copy. The poem may need another scripted pause or two. If I modify it, I will re-send. Does the poem sound somewhat Rumi-lite? My spell check keeps giving alternatives to Rumi.
DT

* * * * * * * * * * * * * * * * * * *

From: Joseph
Subject: Rumi
Date: January 12, 2023 at 1:23 am MT
To: Dennis

I took the liberty of changing "enough grist" to "grist enough". It flows better. Let me know. This was just a first pass. Tempo, drama, ok or better. Suggestions? - As we are dealing with Rumi, I might as well do him justice.

Potter's Hands in Prayer

The Transformation of Mary

She was the butt of village jokes because
Her mind retained its childhood innocence.

She trustingly obeyed him the night
He joined her in her lonely bed, and said,
"This act and this message are from God."

From that moment on,
she was a maid transformed.

The villagers marveled at the birds
Alighting upon her hair.
They doubted their eyes as pebbles rolled aside
Before her bare feet touched the Earth.
They gasped at the cherry trees
Bending down to meet her hungry hands.

The strange girl of the village
Grown stranger still.

But, no longer
Did they laugh.

In Need of a Wife

An oily doily rests upon my little bedside stand.
I must acquire a willing wife to make it clean again.
I will search the wide world o'er, til I find a wife so true.
Who with her busy hands will make my doily look brand new.

I have a mismatched pair of socks where my toes are peeking through.
I wonder, will my blushing bride know what she must do?
Will she mend the holes with softest yarn and mate the mismatched pair?
And after, will she scratch my back, and run fingers through my hair?

Will she always be content to mind her P's and Q's?
Or will she be the type of wife who sometimes brings bad news?
Will she frolic with the Postman while I am Christmas shopping?
Will she dally with the Milkman? Will he offer her creamed topping?

I know that wives bring trouble, and they have since Adam's fall.
Perhaps my little doily isn't oily after all.

The Troubled Knight

He stands naked in the waterfall.
Thank God, it is a sunny day.
He prays no one will see him.
Can this torrent wash his sin away?

The deafening roar,
The blinding spray,
He's heard it said:
The Bible says —
"Water washes sins away".

If that is true, he'll stand here
Naked, for an hour; for a day;
Stand here under Heaven, praying:
Let this water wash my sin away

He recalls the Lady's words:
Our Holy Bible says it plain:
Eye for an eye. Tooth for a tooth.
So, it must follow, as night the day,
The means for casting sin away
Is a sin for a sin. Yes! Sin for sin!
Then you will be Grail Knight again.

He is Christ's own Grail Knight.
What bought him by this way?
He thought to ask a bite to eat.
It was never his intent to stay.
What demon bade me stay?

He crossed a blood red moat,
Red from the morning glare.
At a window of the Castle
He saw a vision fair.
Through the morning mist
He spied an Angel standing there.

The Castle's stately Lady.
That's who invited me to stay.
She ordered me up a banquet.
It's so seldom that a Grail Knight
Comes passing through this way!

She said, *my Lord is not at home.*
He's gone to fight the Horde.
He would say I'm quite remiss
If I did not offer hearth and board.

And it will be quite comforting
To have a Grail Knight near.
I have an only daughter, and
It gets quite lonely here.

She introduced to me her daughter
Who had cheeks of cherry bloom.
Who touched her lips to my left ear,
And whispered of a room.
All to myself, good Grail Knight.
In Tower West I have a room.

And in this room all to myself,
There are rushes on the floor.
My bed is cold and lonely.
And there's no lock upon my door.

Was I tempted? No, not I.
My vows of chastity
Protect me from bold women —
Alas! Not from simple girls like she.
I did not know, how could I know
The world holds girls like she?
As impulsive, yet, as innocent as she?

In the hour after midnight,
I stumbled from her room,
The room without a lock.
I staggered through the gloom;
The chilly gloom of Tower West.

I wandered into Tower East.
Beneath a door I saw a light.
And there! The Castle's Lady
Keeping vigil through the night.

She said: *Come in, young Knight,*
I can sense your heart's in pain.
Come gentle to my breast, dear one.
Come here — confess your sin.

For I'm a Mother, like your Mother.
And we Mothers know what's best.
Come lay your head upon my lap,
And I will give you rest.

I will also give you penance, for
God has graced me with the power
To purge you of your sin.
To restore your knightly flower.
And it will only cost an hour.

Our Holy Bible says it plain:
Eye for an eye; tooth for a tooth.
Surely it follows, as night the day,
The means for casting sin away
Is a sin to erase a sin!
Then you will be Grail Knight again.

And after, I will show the path
Back to your childhood home.
To your anxious Mother's arms.
To your land of ice and stone.

And please, my brave young champion,
If tonight I serve you well,
Give me your oath as Grail Knight,
That our sin you will not tell.
Our sin, you must not tell.

And forever in this lifetime,
To spare us memory and pain,
Do not approach my Castle.
Never cross my blood-red moat again!

Mary and Elizabeth

But I'm not ready to be a mother!
I'm still a teen-ager.
I want to go to lots of weddings.
I want to dance the hora!
I want to sing! Hava nagila! Hava nagila!

Arms above her head,
Hands entwined,
She twirls and twirls,
Her skirts billowing.

Well, it's too late now, cousin.
The bun's in the oven.
So, just between us girls,
How was Joseph?

I'm telling you the truth!
It wasn't Joseph.
It was the Holy Spirit.
That's what the Angel Gabriel said.

Ok. Play it your way, cousin.
But even so, you must tell me everything.
Everything!

Mary performed one final pirouette.
Then they scooted their chairs together.

Suspicious Minds

His friends had their suspicions.
None of them liked the new wife
Who he married after the death of Matrix.
The too-young wife with no apparent history.

She was so remote and controlling.
She did not entertain, nor would she visit.
Matrix had been a sparkling hostess.
Then, before a year had passed, he was dead.

I sent his corpse to an out-of-town funeral home,
The new widow reported, offering no name.
A cremation urn graced the memorial service.
The widow didn't weep. She hired a keener.

Is Grandpa in there?
Ah, the innocence of the young,
Asking the question they couldn't ask.
Is he in there?

Or, is he in the landfill?
Or in the back yard under the new statue of Mary?
Perhaps in Chile, waiting for her and the insurance money?
Is he, perhaps, there?

But hell, this was just crazy thinking.
Why, Doc Folger had signed the death certificate!
They felt bad about their suspicions, and debated
Starting a Go Fund Me account for the new widow.

In six months, the house was sold and she was gone.
Fred, the policeman, had connections at the airport.
Sure enough, she had left town on a jet plane.
The ticket was to Montreal, by way of Cleveland.

When Doc Folger traded up for a Cadillac,
The chatter started up again. You know?
A flight from Montreal to Mexico City,
A diversionary hop to Rio,

Then it's hell for leather, straight to Chile!
That's how it was done, no doubt about it!
But who had time to fly to Santiago to check?
So, for now at least, they let the matter rest.

Funny Girl

In those days, Doctor, I worked for the County.
I was between marriages, and often had my
Saturdays free, so I would spend time in the
Carnegie Public Library of a nearby metropolis.

And that's where I first saw her. The funny girl.
She had blonde hair, and it was close-cropped.
For some reason, I thought she was a library aide.
But she could have been a volunteer, or she could
Have been just a helpful patron.

In any case, she was rushing about among the stacks,
Trying to assist an elderly woman in searching for a book.
It wasn't going well, and the blonde, who looked about
My age, and barely made it into the classification of cute,
Was wound tighter than a spring, racing here and there.

She made an imprint on my mind that is as clear today
As it was forty years ago, when I first saw her.
I think it was because she was in a frenzy in that
Haven of ultimate calm — a public library.

The second time I saw her was on a blind date, arranged
By a consultant who lived with his wife in a restored
House in the metropolis. A nice girl that Nancy knows,
Was all he told me. She was the girl from the library.

And she was still blonde, and was still borderline cute,
And was still wound tighter than a spring. We four
Had our double date. We drove to a nearby outdoor
Festival, and did something while there.

The only snatch of dialog I remember from the whole
Damned evening was Blondie saying, I need a vacation.
For some reason, I got the idea that she might be
Wanting to go on a trip to Cancun. Maybe with me.

I can't remember If we had a follow-up date.
But if we did, I know for sure there was no third date.
She had her own little house, either rented or owned.
Just another someone who you meet, and
Then you wonder about from time to time.

From: Joseph
Subject: Re: Artist Mode
Date: December 29, at 2:43 am MT
To: Dennis

Dennis:

How long have you thought of yourself as an artist? Have you ever thought of yourself as an artist?

It is abundantly clear to me that the muses talk with you regularly. For you to say that you write poems to amuse yourself, is to do do yourself a gross injustice.

I have several friends whom I meet occasionally and talk with about various subjects. One of them is a New York Times war and conflict zone photographer.
He is probably one of the few who has some idea of what goes on as I write and shoot. But even he admits that he is not an artist. Merely willing to go where angels fear to tread, and do his work.

What that means for me is that there are few people, if any, I can talk to seriously about what is going on inside as I am doing my work, shooting in the field, compiling a book or even thinking about what is next. On the other hand, you would understand all of that, and probably more.

I think many of us spend our lives going from day-to-day, making things work the best we can. There are others, and I am sure you are one of those, who ponders and wonders about things that don't appear physically or for which words can barely express.

In your case, you actually are able to express them beautifully. It's the old phrase slightly twisted 1000 words or less is a picture. Which in my case is the opposite, hopefully.

So, I have no picture, at this moment (but, I shall look) to go with The Transformation of Mary. I'm still not sure about including my photographic work in the thing we are doing.

But, your poetry draws all the pictures needed.

Joseph

Swami

Time Traveller: India

After sitting, eyes closed, in the lotus position
For three hours, I felt my body levitating.
Hurry! I yelled to Anna.
Open the damn window!

Which she did just in time for me to float out.
I'm off to India to consult with the Swami,
I called from the far horizon.
Will you be late for supper? Anna called.

I don't know, I called back, as
The curvature of the Earth
Caused my body to disappear.
Would you keep it warm in the oven?

I'm not keeping it forever.
If you're not back by bedtime,
I'm setting it out for the raccoons.
The woman has no soul.

Coroner

He took the small whisk broom
From his right rear pocket
And brushed the dirt from
The emerging face.

Yes, his greatest fear
Finally coming true.
It was Baby Sister, missing
For three months, now.

Of course, it was a ruined face,
But he was a trained Coroner,
And putting two and two together
Was just a day's work for him.

He would have to tell Mother.
He motioned to the photographer,
Who began taking the pictures.
The pictures he would not show Mother.
Even if she asked.

Chapter Five

Appalachian Christmas Memory

It was the leanest Christmas in a long string
Of lean Christmases. Mama made us stay up
All night that Christmas Eve. She was too poor
To buy the soap powder to wash our sheets,
And we always wet our beds on Christmas Eve.

It was the year that Mama cooked a
Little field mouse for our Christmas Meal.
She stuffed it with an acorn.
As I recall, I got a leg.
Jennie got the liver and the gizzard.

It was the year that Mama sent us kids into the town
To beat up every boy and girl we could find;
To steal from every store;
To vandalize the churches.

Roscoe, the Town Cop, couldn't keep up.
Every five minutes his pager would sound.
It's one of them Thompson kids!
Someone would scream.
We were like the Biblical Plague of locusts that year.

You see, we had a coal burning stove,
And we were in great need of coal, and
Mama truly believed that Santa Claus
Brought coal to bad little boys and girls.

Mama worked the Christmas Eve shift
At Bob's IGA Market, because nobody else would.
She made enough money to buy us ten kids
A Christmas Present. Just one.

We took turns opening it.
We took turns acting surprised.
It was a lump of coal. Mama used it
To cook the Christmas Mouse.

Papa? Naw, Papa didn't visit for supper
On that Christmas Night. Mama would of
Whupped his ass.
That kind of Christmas.

Mama gave all us kids hugs when she
Put us to bed on Christmas Night.
It had been quite a day.
We were all stuffed with Christmas Mouse
And hard candy shoplifted from Bob's Market.
Everybody got a hug, because hugs were free.
She was a hugging-Mama. That kind of Mama.
Best Mama I ever knew.

Astro Boy

The Dissimulator

He awakens from his afternoon nap
And wonders: Should he resume
Reading the book on Thomas
Jefferson, that has turned into
Something of a slog?

He hates to be a quitter, but life is
Limited, and stacks of books await.
And yet...this book, though dense,
Has piqued his interest.
He decides to continue for awhile,
But perhaps to do a little skimming.

The author has taken a fresh look at
The famous Virginian:
Our third President;
The Governor of Virginia;
Principal drafter of
The Declaration of Independence;
Architect of Monticello and
The Louisiana Purchase;
And the list could go on and on.

The author argues that Jefferson's
Actions did not match his philosophies.
Tom espoused the beauty and value
Of the small farm, the yeoman way of life.
Yet his political actions promoted
The growth of plantations and
The enrichment of the planter class,
Of which Tom was a member.

The author says that while Tom
Opposed the concept of slavery,
His political deeds actually
Extended the geographic range
And the lifetime in years of that
Cultural nightmare.
In short, Tom was a dissimulator.
Do as I say; not as I do.
Don't feel bad, Ghost of Tom.
We are cursed with such politicians,
Even today.

And, of course, I have to bring
This down to human scale, and
I am thinking of our Tom's
Relationship with Sally Hemings.
Current historical research insists:
There was a Relationship.
(With a capital 'R')

And my mind's eye cannot
Help but see Tom and Sally
Between those damp, homespun
Cotton sheets, and they are
Discussing Sally's promised
And greatly desired freedom.

And Sally, her twice a week
Mission accomplished, asks
When, Tom? When?

And Tom, fully sated, answers:
Next year, Sally, next year.
And call me Mr. Jefferson.

And since I am not a philosopher,
But just a rhymeister, I will conclude
With this little couplet:

Thomas Jefferson was sneaky.
Tom's bedroom stairs were very creaky.

His family looked the other way
When Sally Hemings came to play.

The Settlement

Throughout their growing up years,
Everyone expected them to marry.
And, in time, they did marry.
His inherited wealth and her beauty
Made them the obvious pair.

What everyone did not foresee
Was their separation, less than
A year into the marriage.
"He's impossible!" She said.
He kept his own counsel,
As any Southern gentleman would.

Her father, old General Icarius, he of the
Bulging eyes and bulbous nose, said,
*"She's a little princess, that's what she is.
My little minx will carry water for no man!"*
He then lit his cigar and sipped his scotch.

A year passed, and there was no divorce.
Three more years passed; still no divorce.
"She won't listen to reason," he said.
Each January he deposited a generous
    Stipend into her account.

The women that he knew, and he knew many,
Circled about him like sharks, flashing their
Shark teeth, eyeing him with their shark eyes.
The settlement, you know, he would say.
As soon as she settles, we can marry.
Then he helped himself to their delicacies.

He's still being impossible! She told her many
Male admirers, who waited on their Penelope.
First, the settlement; then I can marry again.
Until then, there is no 'us' for you and me.

    The years of their youth passed, and
        The settlement dragged on.

We are trying, they both insisted.
So they remained free, yet not free.
On the cusp of available, yet not quite so.

Each year they met at the Peabody Hotel in Memphis.
Only to discuss the settlement, you know;
And to reminisce about their one year together.
Correction: Their almost one year together.

It was good, wasn't it? he would alway say.
And every damned time, she would
Take a long sip of her martini and eat an olive
Before answering:

Yes it was good. But this is so much better.

Geronimo

Geronimo's Ghost

In my young days, I took many scalps.
To my mind, it was justified.
They took many acres. They took many buffalo.
They killed my wives and took my dreams away.
We took many scalps.
A trade. They had little else of worth.

Yes, for many years, I was an uncaught Indian.
A creature of beauty; a thing to fear.
What would you give to be an uncaught Indian?
A creature of beauty; a thing to fear?

But I grew weary. Arizona is a harsh land
When you are constantly hunted.
I became a Reservation Indian,
Enjoying an occasional whisky and a cigar
With the Post Commander as we
Reminisced over the old days.

During my life as a Reservation Indian,
I became quite famous.
I rode in the great parade honoring
President Theodore Roosevelt.
I toured with Pawnee Bill.

Even today, over one hundred years
After my departing, I am remembered.
There are two stories of my death.
One story says that I fell asleep
In a drunken stupor, under the stars,
Caught pneumonia and died.

The other is that I fell from a horse,
Was injured and developed pneumonia.
Either way, I was dead, and on my way
To becoming the stuff of legend.

Because the medicine wheel always turns,
Today the disrespectful use of
Indian names has become a cause celebre.
Among some Indians and some whites.

They insist on erasing the word *squaw*
From our sacred mountains.
Arizona's Squaw Peak is no more. Good.
It was truly an insult to our women.

And as for the term *redskin,*
Goodby, Washington Redskins.
May you never win the Super Bowl again.

I find no insult in the name, The Atlanta Braves.
May the Atlanta Braves win many pennants.
May the Cleveland Indians win one now and then.
The tomahawk chop bothers me not at all.

And they must never ban the screaming of
Geronimo!
When our brave American warriors
Parachute from the skies.

Be careful how you trifle, my friends!
In my young days, I took many scalps.
Remember this and be careful.
I might arise — I have the power —
And take many scalps again.

Housing Problem

When we started out, we two,
In our one-room shack,
I saw you every day.
I was happy that way.

In time, we rented
A two-room flat, and
Still plenty of you-me time.
My life was sublime.

Remember our first
Three bedroom rancher?
You took one bedroom for your own.
My first time for sleeping all alone.

We succeeded beyond our wildest dreams.
The house we own today
Has endless, empty, undiscovered rooms,
I wander them, as if among the tombs.

I walk from room to room, and do you know?
It has been years…Years!
Since our paths have crossed.
Oh, the life we've lost!

Our Twins

I gaze upon the sleeping pair.
One is dark; the other fair.
One has curls that shine like gold.
Her twin has hair of blackest coal.

Tonight a fairy gave to me
The un-sought for ability
Their earthly futures for to see.
The secrets of their destiny.

The fairer one will walk in light.
The dark one dance at black midnight.
The fairer one will live for good.
The darker one will curse the Rood.

The fairer one will dress in silk.
The dark one bathe in witch's milk.
The fair one lives for holy deeds.
The dark one nurtures hemlock seeds.

One day they walk beside a stream.
I see their ending like a dream.
The fair one shoves the dark one in.
I did not want to be a twin.
To kill a witch is not a sin.

Sheila

Amanda

Whenever she went to a bar, solo,
She parked her jeans on a stool.
Stag girls sitting alone at a table were
Already the weak hand in the relationship.

Howdy, little girl. Ain't you got no
Friend tonight? Mind if I park here awhile?
Soon as I finish this brand new half gallon
Mug of Pabst, I might just spring for the next round.

Sitting on a bar stool, if you
Need to ditch a loser, you simply
Spun in the other direction and
Prayed for better luck.

If he's a loser too, why,
You just chat up Roscoe, the
Bar man. And Roscoe will play
His part so you'll keep buying drinks.

But tonight's guy, to first appearances,
Is not a loser. Clean shirt,
Clean jeans, clean boots.
One discreet tattoo on his wrist.

I'm Amanda. Hi. Just a
Simple introduction. A few
Words are exchanged, and then
He gets the treatment.

Not to brag, but I'm not
Just any Amanda. I'm the
Amanda that inspired the song.
Amanda, light of my life. That song.

I was sitting on a barstool, just like
We are sitting now. A bar in
Tulsa. And who sits down
Beside me but Don Williams.

Don Williams, the gentle giant
Of country music. The Mellow voice.
Don's dead now, bless his soul:
but not in the hearts of America.

Don was between sets, roaming
The floor, signing autographs.
He signed my napkin, and
Then he signed my shirt.

Yep. Right where you're looking.
But he was a gentleman.
Made me stretch the fabric tight,
And held the pen with three fingers.

Don was wearing that old beat-up
Fedora. He let me in on a secret.
Said he had his hats made to order
At Nudie's. Holes, rips, stains and all,
Custom tailored. Would you believe?

Don stopped doing autographs for
The rest of his break. Couldn't
Tear himself away from me.
Damn, little girl. I'm married,
Were his parting words.

In six months, his song Amanda charted.
The very next year, Old Waylon
Recorded Amanda, and took it
To the top of Billboard's Hot Country.

But Waylon's version didn't have
The rhythm sticks.
That's what made Don's
So special. Those clicking sticks.

The rest of the evening,
Don made it plain he was
Singing to me. Those soulful
Eyes glued on me, his Amanda.

But Don was a family man. Two kids.
Same woman for fifty-seven years.
And that's my story, cowboy.
What's yours?

Why, cowboy! You do know the song!
You're right. Fate should have
Made me a gentleman's wife.
Words like that, and one more margarita
Just might get you a dance.

Brave New World

When I awoke this morning
And peeked out the attic window,
I saw that the world had turned dystopian.

At the end of the block, a city bus was in flames.
It was surrounded by a jazz combo, playing
Blues Lives Matter.

I clearly saw our Baptist Minister, shirt off,
Allowing a tattoo artist to inscribe his back with
Mother-fuck you LGBTQ's. In letters of red, no less.

I yelled downstairs: *Mom! What's going on?*
I'm not sure, she yelled back. But you'll
Need a good breakfast. Fried or scrambled?

This is not how my world ends, I decided.
I put on my Sunday suit and a tie.
Found a ancient bottle of Vitalis and

Slicked my black hair into an Elvis pompadour.
Brushed my teeth until they were flashing, and
Prepared to challenge the insanity of America.

la madre y su hija

Child Star

My childhood, Doctor? No bed of roses.
My opera-obsessed Mother
Pushed and pushed and pushed
Until I got one of the children roles in Norma.

Remember Norma, Doctor?
Bellini composing the most beautiful
Aria of them all? Casta Diva.
Do you know that one, Doctor?

And Norma, who was my Mother
In the opera, stood
Over me with a knife,
To slay me for the sins of my father.

Next season, it was Rodelinda.
One of Handel's operas.
And the same damned thing.
Her kid, Flavio, is about to get the knife.

Italian opera, German opera;
In those days, it didn't matter.
Kids were expendable.
In those days, Mothers were tough titty.

Lonesome Cowboy

Ranger's Command

Old Bill's living down in Texas and getting older every day.
And you ain't? The Captain spat in the fire and then
Threw in another hickory chunk.
Reckon I am, the Kid said, *but I got more days to spare.*

You think you do, the Captain said, and spat in the fire again.
Pure amber stream of tobacco juice sizzling in the embers.
Then he took out his chaw, squeezed and shook it,
And put it in his shirt pocket. *Your days are numbered too.*

You boys want some beans? Granny said.
If you do, you're gonna have to let me get at that fire so's
I can hang the pot on the hook.
Can't have you'ns looking up my skirts when I bend over.

The Kid laughed like a jackal, but he scooted his chair aside.
The Captain didn't move. If he wanted Granny, he'd take her.
He didn't want Granny. He seldom fancied women.
He fancied war. He studied war like most men study their dicks.

When the beans were cooked, the Captain said,
Eat those beans, boy. Eat all you can. Ain't no telling
When you'll see another hot meal. We'll be on the run
After the raid. If we can get to Texas, we'll be alright.

The Kid jerked his head at Granny,
And she ladled his bowl full again. Scalding hot beans and
Chilis and a few chunks of rabbit. Granny knew how to cook.
She hoped the boys would leave her at least one bowlful.

The Kid couldn't wait until the cutting and shooting started.
The Captain couldn't wait until he was in command again.
Even if his whole troop consisted of this skinny boy
And an old Granny woman driving the chuckwagon.

As they were returning to their van,
John Junior spat on the sidewalk,
Breaking every rule she'd ever taught him.
He took a double wad of gum from his mouth and
Put it in his pocket.

She wondered, she really did, if these
Historical re-enactments had any
Redeeming value at all.

The Old Confederate

He was an old Confederate.
Not in body, not in experience,
Not in anything but soul.
He cried like a baby in 1954.

That was the year the Supreme Court
Ruled in Brown -v- Board of Education.
Said the blacks and the whites had to
Integrate the schools.

He had a hunting dog that he named
General Stonewall Jackson.
And he lived in a county where,
If you called your dog to supper by that name,
You'd be feeding half the dogs in the county.

That's how bad it was.
I was in the ninth grade that year.
The Year of the Essay.
The year all the kids in the ninth grade

Had to write an essay on their view
Of Brown -v- Board of Education.
To sum up the opinions of those
Wonderfully educated little piglets,

We ain't a-gonna do it!
Was the sentiment.
Except for one.
Me.
My essay said that the Constitution
Is the Law of the Land, and with
The Supreme Court's ruling,
We are a-gonna do it. Have to.

I was persona my gracious!
For several weeks after that.
The whole damned county
Blamed my daddy for raising me wrong.

That boy never got those ideas on his own,
Is what went around. Also going around
Was a petition to strip my daddy of
His hunting dog naming rights.

He could no longer call his dog
General Stonewall Jackson.
So, Daddy did what he had to do.
Changed the dog's name to Luke,
While crying like a baby.

Old Luke said to me, *I'm glad.*
General Stonewall Jackson was
A ton to remember.
And oh yeah, Daddy saved a bundle
On dog food costs.

From: Joseph
Subject: Re: Reflections
Date: January 16, 2023 at 10:03 am MT
To: Dennis

"Where did that come from" you ask. I think I might be able to give you a clue.

And as for therapy, a therapist would look at your work and liken them to a Rorschack test. It would probably shake them in their boots and they would look at you as an annuity. Frankly, there's another answer the Therapists would not consider. Mas tarde.
JC

* * * * * * * * * * * *

From: Dennis
Subject: Re: Reflections
Date: January 16, 2023 at 8:56 am EST
To: Joseph

I love the thoughts and insights. We must have felt a unique connection even at Transy, or the thread of contact would not have held all these years. It grew thin, and threads grow thin, but it never broke.

Another benefit I am getting from these exercises — it is forcing me to evaluate my poetry, and to attempt to bring the poems into categories, instead of letting them just free-float. I find that writing poetry is probably as cathartic as having a Freudian Psychiatrist. For many of the poems I ask myself, 'now, where did that come from?'
DT

* * * * * * * * * * * * * * *

From: Joseph
Subject: Re: Reflections
Date: January 17, 2023 at 2.41 pm MT
To: Dennis

This stuff brings me joy. My thanks to you.

Ah, my friend, you don't understand - it is your works that are inspiring. IF, aided by my voice, your works might uplift, humble, inspire, or amuse an audience that simply refuses to read or otherwise reflect - then job well done. That you see this as sort of a legacy. All the better.

I suspect that all this will actually get some exposure beyond our expectations. Why not?

Bring it on. I think there is a real venue for this Swan Song in Santa Fe. and even in the mountains of Applachia, More work ahead.

More than likely, you have already considered the following.
We have friends and we then have friends.

So few are those who would tolerate much less engage in conversation our unique ourney through this life and the manner in which we choose (or are able) to expose our soul, inner-ness, frailty, what ever you want to call it.

Discussions of weather, baseball scores, Bradley Tanks, classified documents, doctors visits, etc. I can tolerate, but not for long.

So, even after six decades, not only do I find you a lost friend, but one with whom I have now shared thoughts, beliefs, and feelings about this life and the next, in the unique manner of our art and humbleness (no one would ever accuse me of that), and about life as we know it.

Such a gift. The gift that keeps on giving - that's us, for sure.

Dostoyevsky

Dostoyevsky! The prisoner calls.
Dostoyevsky hurriedly pulls up his trousers.
You are taking your virginity in your hands to
Take a crap in this Gulag.

The newly-arrived prisoners as love interest.
The old timers, strutting and preening.
Bower birds building their nests.
Shit as lubricant.

Dostoyevsky hurriedly pulls up his trousers,
Not taking time to wipe.
With what do you wipe in a Siberian Gulag?
The best option is to scoot across a snowbank.

In his mind, Dostoyevsky is composing.
Eventually, when he is released, he will enter
His most productive literary phase.
Like a nova... rising in the east.

Those massive, unending novels that you
Only have time to read if you are assigned
A life sentence in a Siberian Gulag...
Already forming, word for word, in Dostoyevsky's brain.

Kiss Me At Midnight

Chapter Six

The Thinker

Rumi

Rumi, you said we must know who we are
When our Day of Reckoning arrives.

But of which Day of Reckoning
Were you speaking?

The Day of Our Death?
I suppose that day comes first to mind.
But there other Days of Reckoning.

There is the Day of Our Birth.
The day when we must make our first life decision:
Whether to breathe or not to breathe.

Then there is the Day We Discover Mother.
This is the day and moment when we begin
Our journey into awareness.

There is the Day that we make an Existential Decision:
Whether to spend our precious and limited moments
On this Earth reading our Bible, our Quran, our Vedas…
Or watching TikTok dancers.

Or is it, perhaps, the Day We Commit to a Lover?
It is truly a Day of Reckoning when we choose to
Link our future, our soul, our very being to another.

Oh, Rumi! Rumi!
With one short verse you have
Given us grist enough
upon which to ruminate forever!

And yet…praises to the Holy Ones…
So many of your poems remain…

To tease and test our
Minds, our hearts, our souls.

Anne Boleyn's Falcon

In Hampton Court there is a bird
Perched on a bed of roses.
Within its claws, a scepter bright,
It is good Queen Anne's falcon.

Age twenty-five when first they met,
When good King Henry saw her.
No other maid can hold her hem,
Said Harry. *I must have her.*

He offered her great riches
If she would heed his wooing.
And more regal than the jewels he gave,
He presented her a falcon.

Three years of wedded bliss were theirs;
Then whispers came in swirls.
She cannot birth a Tudor prince;
Only puny Boleyn girls.

In time, he lost his patience;
The King grew tired of waiting.
And right beneath his Queen's own gaze,
Took Jane Seymour for mating.

Yet, Henry was compassionate.
He knew the circumstance.
To ease Queen Anne's beheading,
He brought a swordsman in from France.

What did this King feel for his Queen
As she crossed the Tower Green?
To meet her place in history.
The lonely Anne Boleyn.

Arkansas Traveler

I had an awful dream last night;
I heard the roaring of a train;
And then the telephone, it rang.
It was a call from Cousin May.
Tornadoes heading in our way!

The wife and I, we grabbed the kids.
We five in our one bathroom hid.
Rub a dub dub. Three kids in a tub.
Then a mattress piled on top.
Then the Mama and the Pop.

The tornado came; it slammed right in.
It did, in fact, sound like a train.
The engine took me to my knees.
The conductor shouted, *tickets, please.*
Nobody rides this train for free.

Then the wife lets out a moan,
For her three babies now, are gone.
The wind has taken every one.
Yes, with the Angels they have flown.

She recovers little Fran.
I salvage what is left of Dan.
We never did find Baby Nan.
The wind don't care, it took 'em all.
The wind don't care!   It took 'em all!!

Random Acts

Jennifer was placing a fresh diaper on George Jr.
George Sr. was reaching for Jennifer's side of the
Bed, and missing the contour of her body, and her
Soft murmur at his touch.

On another side of Earth, Yuja was worrying
About this year's rice crop, and about her man
Who was beginning to look at her, when he
Looked at her at all, in a most disturbing way.

On a front porch of a Kentucky shack, a
Mangy blue tick hound was licking his balls
And having cloudy memories about the time
He took a bite of the preacher's ass at homecoming.

In a basement in Detroit Rex Allan was
Surfing the Internet for porn, and feeling
Very pleased with himself in discovering that
Some significant porn was available on Etsy.

In Duluth, Dorothy was making plans to
Have her garage wired for the new electric
Car she was planning to buy...the
First in the neighborhood...Yeah!

In various corners of the world, people were
Thinking of breakfasts...eggs sounded good
Today, with an extra cup of coffee before
Heading out to work.

Then, in less than a nanosecond, the Sun,
Which had caused the grass and trees to grow
For untold centuries, let slip an unexpected fart,
Putting an end to all this nonsense.

The Old Guard

The Vision

It is four am, and he is wide awake;
Until suddenly he isn't. He starts to nod,
And since his attempt at writing
A morning poem has gone nowhere,

He closes his laptop,
Kicks back in his recliner,
Covers up with a blanket, and
Shuts his eyes.

After such careful preparation,
Sleep eludes him.
And then he sees,
On the movie screen of his eyelids,

The Indian, on the stolen Texas pony,
Riding hell for leather straight for his house.
He will be wanting sanctuary
For himself and forage for his horse.

Why, it's Looks Twice, his mythic self,
Who has been absent for awhile,
And now he knows why. Looks Twice
Has been rustling horses again.

At the rate he's coming...
He's already half-way across Alabama,
He will be here in time for breakfast.
As he finally dozes off, he wonders,

What will Looks Twice want to eat?
Will he be craving eggs, over easy,
With hash browns topped with
Shredded cheese and onions?

Will he demand Eggo Waffles
With warm maple syrup, and
Butter blended with olive oil
And sea salt — a favorite?

Or like last time, when he
Rode in hell for leather from
Arizona on another stolen pony,
Will he ask for warm oatmeal?

Topped with walnuts and raisins;
A spoonful of brown sugar;
A sprinkle of cinnamon;
A splash of whole milk.

If this keeps happening, he's
Going to have to fence in
Another five acres of
The family farm.

He once asked Looks Twice,
Why do you need so many horses?
And the smart-ass answer
That Looks Twice gave?

Horses are like potato chips.
You can never be satisfied
With just one.

Southern Comfort
Collection

Queen of the Jukebox Rodeo

During her break-out year as a country music star,
She got famous, got married, and got pregnant.
In that order.
By the second year, it was over.

Well, not over, but at a hiatus.
She loved using that word.
It sounded nasty.
My career is at a hiatus.

Nothing else was at a hiatus.
Just as soon as Rex left for his office,
Big Bad Attorney at Law, you know,
She fed the baby and put her down for a nap.

Then she washed the girlie parts,
Slipped into her latest negligee,
And was rip roaring ready when
The milkman made his delivery.

Ted had never had such a route.
Oh, he had seen such stuff in porno flicks,
But, now, he was living one.
His wife, Frankie, suspected what he was up to.

But she really didn't mind all that much.
Because to tell the truth,
There wasn't much juice left at the old juice bar
By the time the Postman got through with her.

But then, Roscoe got promoted to central processing
At the main Post Office, and Frankie's world turned cold.
There was nothing to do but put the bee on Ted.
And she did just that. Twice a night for the next month.

Ted's weight started falling away, and his eyes got baggy.
The ex-country music queen took him into her kitchen,
Cooked him some scrambled eggs, and let him cry it out.
It's all right Sugar, she assured him. *We had our fun.*

By next fall, she had her figure back.
Her big bad Attorney husband was humping his new Secretary.
So she called up her producer, and sure enough, he had a hit waiting.
And just like that, the hiatus was over,
And all was right with the world.

The Phone Booth

Her Letter

Asters in the Fall;
Violets in the Spring.
Do you ever plan to call?
The call is everything.

Do you like my little rhyme?
Oh, the joy that I could bring
If you only once would call.
The call is everything.

Your father thinks me sweet.
Your mother says I'm vain.
Do you ever plan to call?
The call is everything.

I've found another love.
He calls me now and then.
And although he isn't you,
The call is everything.

Child Bride

Silent Animosities Collection

Broken Hearts

You left her, your high school sweetheart.
After dating for years; after saying
I love you, but never in sonnet form.
You left her.

After permitting her, against your will;
After a month's long struggle;
After prayers and cold showers;
To rob you of your precious virginity.

Her Daddy thinks she is perfect.
Her Mama knows she has little faults.
She agreed with her Daddy; feeling
Perfect, until you took the feeling away.

I had my reasons, I hear you say.
We always have our reasons.
Were your reasons reasonable to her?
Did she cry?

Did you know that God keeps a list?
A list of people who might profit from payback?
It's a long list, and God has other chores.
But, be patient. He'll work His way to you.

Summer's Colors

Last Summer's greens were greenest green.
This Summer's greens are mauve.
For in the bleak midwinter time,
You robbed me of your love.

It was the eve of New Year's Day
When your cold letter came.
I should have never opened it,
But cast it in the flame.

For what good comes in letters
Received on New Year's Eve?
Never has heart been lightened.
But many a heart been grieved.

You said your heart had changed,
And you would think no more of me.
You said with time my heart would heal,
And I would think no more of thee.

In time my heart would heal and
I would think no more of thee?
Can wishes stop the Sun?
An impossibility.

And yet, in time my heart did mend.
And I found another love.
Today we passed upon the street,
And the world... it did not move.

We said our brief hello.
We walked on by, and then,
I must admit I had a thought
Of a life that might have been.

The Stare

Step-Mother

When I was nine, Father brought home
A Wicked Step-Mother. *We will be best friends*,
She said in Father's presence. *You will be the
Little sister I never had.*

Yes, she was only ten years older than I was.
When Father went to call in the cows,
She jerked me to the wood stove that was cooling
From supper, and pushed my head in the oven.

*If you give me any trouble at all, you little vixen,
The next time this oven will not be cool. Do I
Make myself clear?* Yes, I whimpered.
Yes What? Yes Ma'am, I replied.

At bedtime, she told Father, *I will give her
A bath and tuck her in. Then you can come
And kiss her goodnight.* That was fine with
Father, for that was one reason he had married her.

While she was scrubbing me, she recited
A little nursery rhyme that went like this:
Sweet little girls will see tomorrow.
Sassy girls will end in sorrow.
Sassy girls can quickly drown
If their Step-Mothers hold them down.

Then, believe it or not, she lifted me out,
Dried me completely, powdered my nubbin,
Slipped me into a soft gown, and
Tucked me into bed.

My Wicked Step-Mother, who I had
Sworn I would never obey, actually
Raised me to be the woman
That I am today.

How did she know, at only age nineteen,
That I was, in fact, a little vixen,
Determined to make her new life
With Father a living hell?

Soulmate

When she passed away,
Time did not stop,
Though I thought it surely must.

And as time passed, and as my
Awareness of the other returned, I saw
That things were not getting done.

I began to find fingerprints in the dust.
Ah! Are those my fingerprints? The trailing finger
Across the table in the hall.

The dishes that I dirtied were sticking around.
The houseplants were beginning to
Make their wishes known.

What kind of soulmate are you?
So fully here, and at the same time
Not here at all.

Not carrying your share of the load!
But observing, observing, and
Quietly whispering such trivialities as:

The dog needs a bath.
Don't you have eyes to see?
Has your nose forgotten its purpose?

I found myself thinking, I am too old
To deal with a new reality.
Reality didn't care. It dropped in every day.

You always asked me to brew the coffee.
Your coffee is better than mine.
Coffee ready? Some wives say 'good morning.'

And so, I pour your cup, and
Place it on the table by your chair.
And later, I say, *Still pouting, I see.*

This ritual has gone on for five years, now.
These days, your cup becomes my third cup.
Am I making progress?

Progress toward what? I think.
Snap out of it! My eldest daughter says.
Her all-purpose cure-all, since watching Moonstruck.

In some ways, I have snapped out of it.
These days, today, the furniture gets dusted;
The houseplants get watered.

By the end of the day, the dishes
Find themselves in the dish washer.
But I confess; I must confess:
Poor Fritz still needs his bath.

So Cold the Night

Haunted

He made his mistake by telling me that
Schubert's Serenade was his
Favorite musical work of any
Genre — classical, country or pop.

From that night on,
I made my presence known
By softly humming
Schubert's Serenade.

I adopted it as my calling card.
Schubert's Serenade.
You introduced me to it, John.
Until you, I did not know its magic.

The uncertainties of why
Things change.   But things
Change. And in time, his
Desire for me changed.

My desire did not waver.
And I was a constant presence.
He could find no way to
Be rid of me.

He gave up doping, drinking, smoking.
He put two dead bolts on his bedroom door.
He joined the Catholic Church and
Had his Priest perform an exorcism.

At bedtime, he put in ear plugs.
Placed a mask over his eyes.
But he had to breathe, and even
The C-pap could not filter away

The faint, lavender aroma
That announced my nightly
Arrival in his darkened and
Twice-locked bedroom.

So he removed the ear plugs,
And he removed the masks, and
He listened for me to say,
I'm here, John…

And, of course, I did not disappoint.
I said, *I'm here, John.* And then I hummed —
As I will, every night, for the rest of his life —
Schubert's Serenade.

The End

and, still, they have
neither seen nor spoken
to each other
in more than 60 years ...

The Authors

Joseph Cosby

Remains in Santa Fe, New Mexico, with his wife, Sheila, and their Standard Poodle, Mondo. He is an author, artist and international portrait photographer

Dennis Thompson
co-author

Remains in the Appalachian Mountains where he was born, close to where his grandparents settled and where his daughter, Amanda, and her two sons, Derek and Logan, and grandson, Leif, now live

Book II

Losers ...
Weepers ...

Introduction to Book II

Both of us agreed that it was
not necessary for us to actually
talk with each other, like ordinary folk.
In fact, to this day,
we have neither seen
nor spoken to each other
in more than sixty years.

Some of our friends might think that
"the other one" is a figment of our imagination(s).
Who is to say?

In our collaborations,
we plumb the depths of our pasts.
We get to share those lingering
holds to our realities without having
to move to a couch or
write a check.
(And coffee is always on the stove).

Much of this work
draws from the lives of those who
came and left as well as
our own stories which
often ran amok.

To be sure, the reader will be
re-acquainted with most of the
characters from Book I as well as
Dante and the Archangel Michael.

Milton Keynes UK
Ingram Content Group UK Ltd.
UKHW052011011224
451808UK00008B/66